I0603416

2

MANGAOHE PUBLISHERS

ISBN 978-0-9864565-4-1

SHIFTED

Good morning, well yes, somewhere in this world it must be morning by now, and that's where I'm writing from.

It's a gentle morning, I hear a few birds, some of them with joyful tunes. I hear the heat pump gently blowing away, shifting its direction. I hear the house cracking as the sun heats up the window frames. Hm, I'll make a cup of tea first.

When I woke up this morning, I noticed I saw things more clearly than before. Different, wider, deeper, partly as something familiar, and partly as something new. No, not because I was drunk the night before, and I even haven't done drugs, ever. Fucking boring, as my Ozzy neighbours would have said, right? I must be boring to them, as I don't speak their language, and as such I don't use the f-word in every sentence. It seems we live in different worlds. I never see them, I only hear them. So close and yet so far away. Sometimes I wonder if they could see or hear me at all. Maybe they could smell me, if ever I'd be close enough. But then again, our worlds may not be close enough.

What I feel is a different reality, like a world with millions of colours, where most people could just see a few hundred. It took me quite a while to get some kind of grip on it. If you'd see me, would you see the same person that I saw this morning, shaving my beard? If I spoke, would you hear me?

In Paris, it seemed, I could see, read and hear a French world, for as much as my high school memory hadn't abandoned me. The world that I experienced surely wasn't the same for them as it was for me. I can read "*Le Passe Muraille*" without too much effort, but listening to a Frenchman explaining about it, is of quite a different dimension, let alone if it were a charming French woman.

When you walk down the 32 steps at *Gare Javel* you may be walking right in her footsteps, and yet you may never know. You could be standing right next to her, waiting for the train to *Château Versailles*, not noticing her warmth. She might as well be a sculpture at the Trocadero. Different realities, different dimensions.

I walked up about ten steps with my camera to see how it would look from there, and came back down. Something had changed but I did not see what. That must have been the first time I had seen Françoise. A simple "*Bonjour*" was all we exchanged while she came up the stairs. For some reason she stayed in my mind for the rest of the morning, and even during my exploration at Versailles, studying gilded window handles or the fake brick facades, she seemed to pop up in my mind out of nowhere. Foolishly I turned around to see if she was there, but in between a few tourists there was no sight of her. Instead I watched the tourists, wondering what they were looking at, or what they were not looking at, as they seemed to move about like a conveyor belt, not noticing the details, the whole of stories within them. In the *Grande Galerie* it even got worse, the "oohs" and "ahs", while the conveyor belt moved on, packing more people into the mirrored sardine can. I stepped to the side and moved my hand with the camera up, taking a few pictures over the crowd. This was, as it later turned out, where Françoise was standing no more than two metres away from me, but I did not see her because of a group of tourists. I saw so much, but I did not see her. I did not know that I had not seen her, but later in the pictures I noticed her... The crowd around me started to make me feel somewhat annoyed, uncomfortable. I needed to move on, so I actually got back into the crowd. Going along with the flow, the noise of a thousand feet slowly moving in one direction and the close by cackling in multiple languages was getting too much, and I hurried towards the next room. That was where I suddenly stood eye to eye with Françoise. It was as if all feet had stopped moving, all voices silenced. "*Bonjour encore*," she said with a lovely smile and a voice to die for.

One

I died. I died and that was where it started. I have a slight headache, I sip my tea and look outside at a man walking past. I notice that the colours have changed, from vibrant green to a dull brownish green. What I see is looking cold and not the warm I expect. Maybe in between, not warm, not cold, more like nothingness. The man comes walking past again, in the other direction.

My tea has slightly cooled so I can take a few larger sips and soon notice my little headache starts to disappear. Françoise comes in. "*Bonjour mon amour*", a hasty kiss and off she is again through the other door, her red dress flaunting after her. I think she is holding something in her hands, but I'm not sure. When she comes back after a minute it seems to me as if the colour of her dress is slightly different than I first thought it was, a warmer red, maybe with a hint of orange.

"It was a ladybird," she says with her lovely musical accent. "You know, a yellow one," and she comes to sit beside me.

"Did you finish your paper?" I ask while pouring a tea for

her too. I had heard a few *merdes*, so I'm not sure what to expect.

"Sure, almost done," she says.

After we finish our teas we go outside, the dull brownish green has changed into a lively warm green, the branches are moving gently in the wind. A monarch butterfly moves swiftly back and forth between the flowers and the trees while we sit down on the deck. I take my last sip of tea, and then focus on the colours to see what state we're in. *Une haute conscience* is my conclusion. The colours are becoming more stable, which means that the higher state of awareness is becoming more stable as Françoise has explained to me. She works at the M-institute, where she actually researches those colour changes.

I have noticed with several people when discussing colours that it seems we were all seeing different colours, sometimes slightly different and sometimes very different. When I see a tint of orange and someone calls it dark yellow, I now know that the more complex colour is the one that belongs to the higher state of awareness. At first the colours I saw would shift between a dark yellow and orange, but as said before, it is far more stable now. Almost increasing by the day. With some people I noticed, very few in fact, it created an invisible connection. I would see them, feel them, I would feel them stand out in a crowd, as if it would be a separate world, within this world, as if higher awareness attracts higher awareness. A friend from Brussels, Edouard Hubert, had noticed during an art show, where I was on the balcony of the first floor, and my daughter was on the ground floor, it was as if there was a visible connection between us. Where I'd move, the connection would move with me. It was a fascinating sight, he said. To me it already felt normal, but was quite surprised to hear that someone else could see it; I mean that the connection, the cable so to speak, would be visible. I wondered how long that cable could be stretched, or if it would grow longer if the distance would become larger?

Two

Right in front of Jacques de Bourbon she asked if I wanted to go outside, and get a drink. So we hunted for the shortest cut outside. It was a wonderful day, a bright blue sky with a few white clouds, a soft breeze that seemed to carry the smell of flowers and a gentle temperature for this time of year. I already had excused myself for my French, so we settled on English, with a teaspoon of French.

There was a stall that advertised hot and cold drinks next to the pond and there was a place to sit close by. I left my bag and my camera at the small table to get us something to drink. When I returned with two green teas I noticed her scribbling in a yellow notebook that she swiftly moved to the side to make room for the mugs. After we had a sip, she introduced herself as Françoise, an art history student, "a modern art history student" she corrected herself. "So then, why here in these old buildings?" I asked.

"It is, ehm, as the context for modern art. Where is it rooted, where does it connect, how does one explain the other?

"And where does modern art start?" she continued after

a few seconds. "And where does it stop?"

We then argued about the art, the fashions and styles that make Versailles, how modern art in a specific period would shift with time, and become not-modern art. Or how copying classic art becomes a different form of modern art, or just a cheap modern fashion. Françoise and I agreed. We agreed as if it was a dance of arguments, complementary moves, a helix into the sunny blue sky.

The elegance of a well-educated, well-spoken, well-dressed French *mademoiselle* never ceases to amaze me. Even in blue jeans, somehow timeless. I started to look at her differently, not just the way she looks, her charm, and wondered, is she as beautiful on the inside as she is on the outside? Does she have a heart, a wonderful heart?

"Which of the many universities in Paris are you studying at?" I asked, in a slightly clumsy attempt to make the conversation more personal.

"*Ah, non*, not here in Paris. I'm studying in Brussels, the *Vrije Universiteit*," she said, again with her warm voice and its mesmerising accent.

"I'm sorry, I thought you were French, ah well, it seems Belgians can be charming too."

She smiled. "Well, *merci bien*, but I am French." Followed

by the cheekiest smiling eyes ever. She leaned over and gave me a kiss on my cheek. "I have to go now." She swiftly stood up. "*À bientôt!*" And she was gone. I was stunned for a moment, then I laughed out loud, it was the weirdest ending of one of the most beautiful conversations ever, or something like that.

I remained on that little wooden bench for a little longer, recapitulating what just happened in that last hour or so. I watched the pond, the ripples in the water, the people on the other side, how vibrant everything seemed! How weird and warm I felt, how utterly weird, warm and comfortable I felt. I walked back to the *château*, looked at its fashionable architecture of grandeur, the powerful yellow in the afternoon sun. It perfectly fitted with how I felt. Then I noticed the foreign tourists, their screaming t-shirts, joggling along. The contrasts could not be more enormous. What did they see? What didn't they see? And then I burst out in another laugh.

I went back to the *Grande Galerie*, to see if it had become quieter and indeed it was. An Asian couple was taking a picture of themselves in the mirrored wall while I walked behind them. I wonder what they'd see in their picture. Would they see me waving? I looked at the ceiling with its slightly dull-coloured paintings amidst the gold coloured ornamentation. Some life-sized golden chandeliers of graciously moving young ladies holding electric lights looked as if they came out of a Chinese mould yesterday. Impressive? Maybe. Amusing? Absolutely.

While continuing the journey the elaborate gold-coloured joinery stood out. The original old ones, and the new copies. I enjoyed watching for little details, as I imagined the people working on them. "God is in the details" as Ludwig Mies van der Rohe would have said centuries later. Every little surface seemed another opportunity for more ornamentation, symbolism, decadence. While old, and worn from hundreds of years of use, the window handles still seemed to be working perfectly, a good investment in proper workmanship, I thought. Looking through the window I watched the bright orange bricks. Different shades of orange and a very fine cement, as if smoothened with a finger, rather than with a tool. No fingerprints left behind, but with some clear, small and delicate stamps in the clay from the brick makers. I noticed "EH" and what seemed to look like "MI", but that was just an "EH" stamp on its side. I wondered for a moment what it would stand for. A little further a door was left open, maybe on purpose for ventilation. I could feel the golden ornament, the *fleur-de-lis*, the little golden shells encircling the stylised shield. It was as if touching through time. It was as if I had been here before. It felt familiar, warm, home. Home. A little breeze got me into the present again. It was quiet, I was alone. As I walked further a large door towards the gardens was open. It was a gentle sight with hardly any tourists left as it was getting later in the afternoon already.

In the evening I met with my wife Joan who was on a conference in Paris, while I was exploring town. We were at the *Gare du Nord*, where I showed her some of the pictures I had made. Freemason symbols, the "LP" doorhandles, and the fake brick facade that was peeling off, showing the reality behind the suggestion... Even though its texture and colour greatly matched the original, real bricks. Next time she'd come with me, she said.

Three

My darling Françoise didn't have any issues with changing colours, her reality of colours got stable a long time ago already. I think I myself got used to the changing colours fairly quickly though, but then again it took quite a while before the colours became stable, into the warmer, more complex colours, that I actually always had liked. "Dirty colours" I used to call them, but now I think of them more as "warm and complex colours". With an exception though, somehow I hardly ever feel warmth with complex blue colours. Even along the coastline of the *Côte d'Azur*, with its astonishing blueish green, or is it greenish blue tints, the colour stays at a distance, as if it can not touch me, as if I can not be touched by it.

The monarch butterfly moves into the protection of the trees as the day comes to a close.

It wasn't until a few days later, that our daughter had come over for the weekend. Marie-Isobelle likes to spend her weekends at our place.

She dances around in the living room without music, as if her life depends on it. Maybe it does... And then she'll take one of my guitars, to play and sing a gentle song, or sit with me, and give me a hug, just out of the blue. Her favourite colour is purple, especially the warmer, deeper shades of purple. It suits her long dark hair, its elegance, like her mother's. Marie-Isobelle lives in Amsterdam, where she studies astrophysics. I think it's kind of cool she didn't follow in either my or Françoise's footsteps, but found her own way. And I think it's cool she spends her time where she wants to be.

Today she seems a bit quiet. As usual she walks with her bare feet over the grass as I watch her from behind my desk. One foot carefully in front of the other, like a ballet dancer, but she's not dancing. Her arms draped along her body, not swinging around, her face down, not up. And then her face goes up, suddenly, as if something had fallen upon her from the sky.

"Papa!" she calls out, while walking with big steps towards the house, "Papa!". She walks on to the deck, into the house, and looks straight into my eyes. "Last week, well just before I left to visit you, there was a Japanese professor at our university." She stops for a moment. "He said he was visiting several universities, to ask students to do a test for his research, students from several different departments."

She explains she hadn't heard his name when he was introduced, and even didn't hear his name after he introduced himself again. Well, she heard it, but didn't exactly remember. "Something with *koda*," she continues.

She then starts to explain how he sniffed the air as if he was smelling something peculiar, and then particularly had turned towards Marie-Isobelle.

"I wasn't sure if I should tell you, but, well, I was thinking about it and realised he might not have asked me by accident."

"Well, what do you mean Mai? What did he ask you?"

"He asked me if I'm familiar with, ehm, dirty colours, and if I liked them."

She points at her blouse and shows how she was wearing that same blouse that day, and that professor "Koda" as she calls him now, had also referred to her blouse.

"Koda..., Koda," it rings in my head. "Koda, what age do you think he is? What does he look like?"

"Well, older than you, a lot older than you actually. Seventy maybe, or more? He wore an old-fashioned suit, orange-brownish, he was short, like this," and Marie-Isobelle raises her hand towards her shoulder. "And he wore glasses," she continues, "round, like yours. I think they were black."

Somehow it triggers a memory, but I can't get a grip on it. Like, when I was a student we had a visiting Japanese professor who..., also asked if we would participate in his research, colour research! He wore dark round glasses, and after we had filled out his questionnaires it turned out that I had the highest score on colour recognition, but I didn't want to stand out, so I kept my score to myself, and nobody noticed...

"Koda..." No, that doesn't ring a bell.

A week goes by and Marie-Isobelle is again at our house. Françoise had prepared a lunch and we all sit at the table. "Papa, do you remember I told you about that Japanese professor at my university?"

"Sure, Koda, right?"

"Yes, Koda. Well no..., his name isn't Koda. His university is in Koda..., Kodaira, oh wait, his name is Kodaira. He has sent me a letter and asks if he can meet me in Amsterdam."

It triggers my protective, caring parent nerves. "Why does he want to meet you, in Amsterdam?"

"He says he's in Amsterdam next week, as he knows from the questionnaire that I live in Amsterdam? I don't know, he said I had an extraordinary score which triggered his curiosity for his research."

Not wanting to be over-protective I try to keep the issue small, and ask if there's more information in his letter. Françoise looks at me while taking another bite from her deliciously filled *baguette*, while Marie-Isobelle wants to take the letter from her bag, but then Françoise tells her, "Leave it for after lunch." Parents...

Four

After we returned home the weather had changed, no longer the bright blue sky, but grey clouds, with only a distant patch of blue. The seasons seemed to be getting mixed up. Instead of the gentle warmth I was expecting, the wind had turned icy, cold, it seemed like another polar blow.

I decided to stay in that day and have a look at all the pictures I had made a few days earlier.

The Eiffel Tower, with *Gare Javel*, scenes out of the train window; "*GARAGE du VIADUC*", a semi-butterfly roof at Val Fleury station, a mechanical toy bird stuck on the top of the gate at *Château Versailles*...

And then there were the lines of people waiting to get in, seemingly endless lines of people, waiting. Some reading tourist information books, some already taking pictures, hm, some watching at each other in lines going in opposite directions. Were they going round and round? Was I going round and round with them?

As it turned out I did come closer to the *château* and the first marvels were starting to reveal themselves. The *fleurs-*

de-lis on top of the chapel reminded me of the coat-of-arms of my own family, the extremely elaborate decoration of wasteful decadence and the conflicting message of religions. The statues of even more vanity as an "appetiser" of what was to come?

It seemed I ended up making dozens of pictures of the interior; the ceiling paintings with gold decoration, an intense mix of beauty and ugliness. I read "*APPENDERUNT MERCEDEM MEAM TRIGINTA ARGENTEOS*", "So they weighed for my price thirty pieces of silver". "Why", I thought, "is it about money in so many houses of God?"

Outside of the chapel I walked through a corridor with black and white floor tiles, natural stones and on the left side a line of statues, in the same colour as the walls, as if they might not get noticed if one wasn't paying attention. A few gold-coloured lanterns hanging from the ceiling and well, that was it. The contrast with the previous space couldn't be larger, I truly enjoyed and preferred the last one, but then again, not least because of the immense contrasts with the chapel.

This was also where I noticed the first golden "LP" ornaments on the plate glass doors, new ones as it turned out later. Through the doors there was a great view onto the inner courtyard, and the weathered facades of the other rooms and spaces around it. While my pictures were showing ever more shiny gilded details, I also noticed a dramatic increase in the amount of tourists, so much so that I also started to take pictures of them, like adding an extra dimension to the beauty and ugliness I already was experiencing. Most of their heads were lifted up towards the ceiling, it looked a bit silly actually. Then came a very narrow corridor, well, it was only narrow because of the amount of people getting through, onto the *Grande Galerie* or the Hall of Mirrors. And on the very next picture, where I had raised my camera, pointing over the crowds, I saw Françoise, looking straight into the camera. I did not see her then, but had she seen me?

In the next room, in front of Jacques de Bourbon, just after I had taken a picture of the bust, was where I suddenly stood eye to eye with Françoise.

Did she know I was coming? Was she waiting there for me? I didn't realise it then, but "I know now", I thought.

As if that picture in the *Grande Galerie* wasn't enough, the next picture was even more surprising. Maybe mesmerising is the better word. It was a picture of her yellow notebook, a page where she had written a message for me, I thought.

"Wednesday, March 26th, 3:00 PM, Keizersgracht 324, Amsterdam. Meet me on the roof. F."

What does a grown-up man do in such a case? Jump in his car and race towards Amsterdam. But I wasn't just a grown-up man, I was a grown-up, married man, and the 26th of March was still about a month away... "Why me? Why now? Why then?"

In the next few weeks it kept puzzling my mind. I felt uncomfortable when I discussed it with my wife as I didn't exactly know what this was about. I didn't know what to expect, from Françoise, nor from my darling wife. When the 26th of March was coming closer and closer I became more restless. Restless but yet still feeling good, not sure, but there was something utterly good going on, I felt. Or was it? Almost every evening I would have a look at the pictures to see what I might not have seen. Were there other people in those pictures that I should have seen? I could not get it out of my mind.

Joan seemed perfectly comfortable with the idea, and yet for me doubt was continuously rising. "What was I thinking?"

It was the 23rd of March when she said with a smile "Why don't you just go?" The next day I decided to go and on the 25th I went.

On the highway my mind drifted away with the clouds, it looked as if rain could fall any moment, but it didn't, and on the radio I heard Katrina singing "I'm walking on sunshine", right when the sun burst through. I smiled, I put my worries and doubt aside and decided to enjoy the journey. Closer to the border of the Netherlands the traffic became more intense, was there a big sale event going on that I didn't know of? Closer towards Amsterdam it only became worse and my joy started to wear off. Was I really doing the right thing?

After a few minutes I stopped at a resting place next to the highway. With the engine off, I took a deep sigh and looked into the abyss for a few moments. Somehow I felt a largeness to my journey that was beyond the scale I was familiar with. Somehow I felt comfortable, relaxed, even excited, somehow I felt alert, and still this nagging sense of "Am I doing the right thing?"

An old man came walking up to my car, leaned down towards the passenger window and I lowered it. "This has always been my dream car," he said. A little bit set on alert I paid attention to his moves and even more when he seemed to study the interior. "I've never seen it with these red seats, they look great. And I love the sound of that engine, it's converted to hydrogen I guess?" I confirmed it was.

"And those are solar panels, right?"

"Indeed, they are high density."

"I like how they made them look like classic sport stripes on this *grigio* paint."

He asked if it was OK for him to take a few pictures and I told him to please go ahead while I got out of the car. While he walked back to his own car, I walked up to the restaurant to get me a cappuccino.

I took two of those long, narrow sugar sachets and put them on top of each other, in opposite directions, and tore off the ends. Then poured out the sugar and gently pushed one sachet inside of the other, till they seemingly formed a new, filled sugar sachet. Then I put it back in the box between the others. With a full exchange of fluids I got back into my car and started the engine. It was a great sound alright. "Amsterdam, here I come."

The next morning I woke up in a small, but modern and luxurious hotel room, got dressed in my usual casual-smart and green, and walked out to get me some breakfast.

Hm, I loved this city, I always did, but even more so in

recent years. Maybe it's because when you get older, you learn to see things with different eyes, you learn to appreciate things with different eyes. But then again, this city also has grown older with time, and changed. It changed itself and it changed people, in changing relationships. While enjoying the coffee I watched the people move by, silently, still mostly on manpowered bikes which clearly has had a continuous effect on the physical health of Amsterdam's population. After I had finished my breakfast, I got up and walked towards the direction of the Keizersgracht. There's an elegance in those seemingly hovering bikes that adds to this city, something timeless... "Oh wait, what time was the meeting at the Keizersgracht?", as I realised I wasn't just here to observe the pretty hovering bikesters... I looked on my watch and noticed there was plenty of time though, for all of it. The next moment something zapped right in front of my eyes... "Sorry!", she yelled and moved along on her yellow bike. Oops, that was a bit too close for a safe observation. Where was I exactly? "Gravenstraat, Nieuwezijds Voorburgwal" said the signs on the sides of the corner. Every time I've been to Amsterdam those little shops built against the walls of the "Nieuwe Kerk" claimed my attention, sometimes there was a shop in them, sometimes they were just sitting empty, as I fantasised what kind of business would fit in them. An art shop? A proper coffee shop? I went straight ahead towards the Molensteeg. There was no traffic when I crossed the road, though somewhere near I heard a slightly alarming noise of a high-revving engine, but didn't see anything. Along the Molensteeg I noticed the well-maintained facades, warm and full of character, inspiring like so many small businesses here I thought. A few moments later, on the Torensluis bridge, I stood eye to eye with Multatuli. He made me go back and grab a coffee at the nearest cafe. While I waited for my coffee I reflected on Multatuli, or Eduard Douwes Dekker as I remembered from high school. His novel "Max Havelaar" was a story about the old Dutch coffee business but more essentially about corruption and organised crime. As such it was of great influence on my thinking as a young student, not that I had actually understood much of it then. I very much enjoyed my coffee though, outside, in the middle of this mild day in the end of March. In the distance, for a few moments I heard that engine noise again, but now it did come closer. I watched a dark, shining dot on the other side of the canal, coming closer and closer, and soon recognised it as the same 4C as mine, the same colour, same wheels, but with foreign licence plates that I didn't recognise. What a beauty, and great to see it in this light, this background. The engine gently rumbling and the tyres rattling on the cobble stones, or "*kinderkopjes*", as they were called in Dutch. For a moment I thought of taking a picture, but I didn't, and just enjoyed it driving by on the other side, as it was a fairly rare sight to enjoy. Great, just great.

When lunchtime was approaching I headed towards the Keizersgracht again as to make sure I wouldn't be too far away from the meeting place after I'd have finished my lunch. So, on the Leliegracht, just before the Keizersgracht, I found a great-looking restaurant, vegan of course. A lady was sitting in the sun in front of it, but I thought it would be more comfortable inside. I got a menu from the waitress and immediately found the light lunch I was looking for: a sandwich with vegan cheese, pesto, tomato, lettuce and alfalfa.

"Last time I had the homemade brie, it's delicious", said the lady who also had come inside for lunch, and sat right next to me. "Do you mind?" she asked kindly...

"Please go ahead," I said, a little bit overwhelmed. I looked at the menu again, and indeed the "Homemade brie made from almonds, with fig spread, rucola & pint nuts" looked interesting. Hm, "pint nuts"? Really? I decided to try it anyway. It was warm and comfortable behind the large glass window, so I felt like ordering a glass of kombucha. The lady next to me did the same, and she ordered the sandwich with vegan cheese. Hm...

"I'm Agnes," she said with an accent that I could not clearly identify, somewhat American, but without the loudness? "I come here every month to visit my daughter, but she just called that she'll be late, so I should have my lunch on my own. But not anymore!" she laughed.

Our kombuchas were served and we toasted to "not lunching alone!" After we had almost finished our lunch her daughter came in. Agnes introduced us and her daughter sat down next to her and considered whether or not she would still have a lunch. "A sandwich with vegan cheese?" Agnes suggested, as a quick and easy bite... I didn't say anything. Then I noticed it was already later then I expected and left the two ladies, thanking them for our great chat, paid at the counter and was off to the last branch of the journey to Keizersgracht 234. At the corner of the Keizersgracht I asked a waiter for the directions to number 234. "On the other side, to the left," he said.

Already after a few minutes I was standing in front of the

building, a bar actually, and seemingly closed... I looked inside and noticed someone walking and gently nocked on the window. A man opened the door. "We're open from 3," he said.

"And I'm supposed to meet someone here at 3," I said.

"Oh well, you can wait inside if you like," the man kindly suggested. We walked inside and I took a seat at the bar.

"Can I get you something to drink while you wait?"

"Ah, no thank you, I'll wait till my friend arrives. She actually said to meet her on the roof," I said. He looked at me with a sense of bewilderment...

"I'm sorry, but you can't go on the roof. Your friend may have pulled a joke on you, or are you trying to pull a joke on me?"

"No, no, surely not!" I started to feel the planks move from under me... Did I come here all the way for some idiotic joke? I looked again at the note, "3:00PM, Keizersgracht 324". "I'm very sorry, I'm at the wrong number, it should be 324."

"Just a few minutes that way," he said, "you can make it just in time," adding something that I did not understand.

I hurried outside, felt totally stupid, and tried not to let it get to me. "Argh!" Instead of enjoying the walk along the

Keizersgracht I now was filled with doubt and a bit of anger and hardly saw anything of the fascinating canal houses. Just one or two minutes before 3:00 I stood in front of a large building, "Felix Meritis" it said. I walked inside and immediately asked the staff if I could get to the roof, as I'd have a meeting with a friend there. She looked around for a moment and then, as if it was the most normal question ever she said I could get a ticket at the counter. OK I thought, so there was a roof to meet her, and it was a regular thing to do. I got me a ticket and took the lift to the top of the building. Another staircase, and I was under the blue sky...

On the roof I looked around, noticed several tripods and one with a telescope mounted on top of it, and was amazed with the wide view over the canal houses, so different from the view below. I was alone, the wind was a bit chilly and I still thought this could be a bad joke. But then again, I was on the roof, and it was perfectly normal. I calmed down and calmly looked over the fence. Looking down from the top into other people's lives, and looking further away to see glimpses from the contrasting industrial structures towards the horizon. Then I walked up to the telescope and decided to have a look through it. It was pointing slightly towards north-west. I saw a modern, red brick building, with something like a stepped roof. Along the top of the building a light moved from left to right, and then from right to left. Then it stopped.

I waited for the display to start moving again, or to change colour, or for some advertising text to appear. Then out of nowhere the light moved towards me. It was not attached to the building, it moved towards me! And it was speeding up, straight towards me. Just as it seemed to get out of focus it stopped again and moved slightly back into focus. It was hovering in mid-air. I was nailed to the ground, my eye glued to the telescope. I did not dare to look up. Then it slowly moved again, from west to east, hovering in a straight line and I followed it with the telescope, until it disappeared behind another building.

Five

"It seems it's a kind letter, but I'm still not too sure what to think of it. What do you think of it?"

Marie-Isobelle folds her hands and gently knocks them against her chin. "Professor..., oh, I can't remember his name again..., Koda..., Kodaira, seemed like a kind old man, but the way he looked at me felt a bit weird, creepy."

"Maybe he's just fascinated by good-looking young women," Françoise says smiling from behind the bar. "Well you know, who isn't?"

Marie-Isobelle smiles and leans back, her hands now relaxed on the table. "OK, good-looking mother!" With a smile Françoise sticks out her vibrant, light turquoise tongue.

I take another look at the letter while Françoise comes back to the table with a few glasses. "What you could do is indeed meet him, but do it in a quiet, yet clearly public, open and light place. Something like that restaurant next to the Dam where we were last time."

"I think I agree with your mother," while I look to see Marie-Isobelle's response.

"OK, then I'll do that," and she raises her glass for a toast. "Cheers!"

Four days later Marie-Isobelle sits on a terrace under the blue sky, on a roof, next to the Dam. She has chosen a table in the middle, in the shadow of a large potted tree. A gentle summer breeze plays with her hair while she listens to professor Kodaira. The waiter serves tea for one, and an orange-mango juice for the other.

"I've started this research decades ago," he says. "In the beginning we just did it in Japan, but soon learned to do it in other countries as well. From our early research we found that people believe that they all see or think of the same colour when it is concerning the colour yellow. On the one hand people do see different colours because they have a different sensibility to colours, on the other hand people see different colours but learned the same word for it. For example, you may grow up seeing the colour blue, but learning the name "red" for it, and for the rest of your life believe you're seeing the colour red, while seeing the colour blue. And there never is a misunderstanding about colours, because everybody sticks to the word they learned for each individual colour. The difference shows itself however when people have a preference for a colour, or colour combination that is very different from yours, even where you might think that's a very ugly colour combination." He pauses for a moment, takes a sip of tea, while Marie-Isobelle listens carefully. "The main goal of our research however," he continues his little lecture," is that first group. And that is where you come into the picture."

Marie-Isobelle now also takes a sip from her glass. "So, what you're saying is that we may not be seeing the same colours right now, like for this juice?"

"Yes, and I expect that you see a far more complex colour than what most people see, or even what I see."

"Wow, but ehm, I don't know what that means."

"It means, that we think that your general awareness is higher than 1 in 10,000 people, probably more closer to 1 in 100,000 people, or even more, a million? But despite the scale of our research we haven't interviewed enough people yet to make such a statement. We try to get more funding, but it's still very hard to get funding for research that does not seem to be commercially exploitable, even though it seems to be getting better."

The colours are changing, it seems they are going back and forth between dirtier and cleaner. Marie-Isobelle is not entirely comfortable anymore.

"I see this is making you feel uncomfortable?" professor Kodaira asks.

"A little bit, I didn't know exactly what to expect when I came here, but now it feels I'm suddenly already in the middle of a project that I did not choose to participate in. Or something like that."

Professor Kodaira stops talking, Marie-Isobelle starts thinking.

"I know about the colours," she says, "I know about the different shades of colours for different people, well, just about the different shades and how they may be changing." She pauses for a few moments. "Do you see, I mean, did you just see the colours changing?"

"Yes I did, they shifted between dirty and clean, a few times, and back to dirty, right?"

"Yes, I know most people can not see it, but that's changing, right? I mean, more people are seeing more colours, right?"

"Yes," professor Kodaira confirms again. "But there is more to it."

Marie-Isobelle leans a bit forward, as if she doesn't want to miss a word of what professor Kodaira will be saying next.

"What we talked about till now, was about passive colour changes. What I'd like to talk about with you is about active colour changes, shifting colours at will."

Marie-Isobelle is all ears. The world around her seems to stop moving.

"Shifting colours at will is not as simple as it seems," professor Kodaira continues, "it is more like a secondary effect of a mood change. You change the mood, and the colours follow. So I mean, it's not just a passive thing, it's much more, I think, like with you."

Professor Kodaira studies Marie-Isobelle with fatherly care, while Marie-Isobelle leans back, and reaches for her glass. She raises it and watches it carefully while lunch is being served.

After the somewhat late light lunch Marie-Isobelle walks back to her apartment and calls home. Françoise connects, and Marie-Isobelle tells her the whole story.

"And for this evening he invited me for dinner with his daughter, who is the owner of a designer-bag shop here, her name is Chisato Kodaira."

The evening is getting filled with colours; bags of different colours, stars of different colours, people of different colours and moods of different colours.

Chisato Kodaira is very kind, well-educated, well-informed, well-dressed, but the only thing that isn't clear about her is her age. Mature and youthful, focused and playful, delicate and strong. Clearly her father is very proud of her and they both enjoy each other's presence. Her mother died when she was young, and her father raised her on his own. Marie-Isobelle already had noticed that Chisato's tongue is warm purple, like hers. She feels connected.

After dinner they decide to have a look at Chisato's shop that is only a short stroll away. Professor Kodaira walks a few steps behind them while the two women seem to be engaged in a highly tuned conversation. When they reach the shop Chisato opens the door and they go in, not noticing that professor Kodaira is not walking behind them anymore.

Six

I looked up from the scope, but saw nothing. Behind me I heard a voice. "*Bonjour!*" she said, while I turned around.

"Did you just see that!" I asked.

"No, I didn't, it was just for you," she said.

Then I realised I was here to meet her.

"So, you knew about this? You knew this would happen? What was that?"

"UFO, OVNI, light orb, Von Neumann probe, foo-fighters, you name it, we got it.We refer to them as Sentinels."

"Who is 'we'?"

"'We' are my friends and I who know about the phenomenon," Françoise replied.

"Did you make me come for this?"

"Yes..., and for this." And she stepped closer and gave me a warm hug, a kiss, and a warm hug.

Still holding me, she leaned back a bit, looked me in the eyes and said: "I'm so glad you came. How are you? I was waiting downstairs, but you did not see me. The waitress noticed you, you were in a hurry and she let you go up by yourself after she checked with me. I'm so glad you came!"

I did not realise how impressed I was with her voice, like as if the timbre resonated with each fibre in my body.

"I'm glad I came Françoise, and I'm glad to see you too, but an entrance with a little introduction would have done nicely too. What is this about? Or what was that about?" I felt slightly bewildered, the mix of emotions of this experience, and seeing her again. Holding her.

"You needed to see her on your own, experience it on your own, clean, open-minded, without prejudice. And so you did, because she came to you. I always say 'she', but I don't know, she behaves likes a kind woman," she said with a smile. "And how are you?" she asked while taking my hand to sit on the little bench.

After some fifteen, twenty minutes, it even might have been a lot more, Françoise suggested to go downstairs and get something warm to drink, and to meet two of her friends. It felt as if I was in a slow rollercoaster of introductions. While we went down, a lot of other people came up. Did she arrange for us to be alone? We took the stairs down instead of the lift, she clearly was familiar with this place. The old timber staircase looked as if it had been installed yesterday, shiny and smooth, the interior was a pleasant mixture of old and new. While we kept climbing down the stairs, going round and round, I noticed how she kept smiling, and often turned her head towards me when she walked down the stairs next to me. She took my hand again and I felt like in a dream, as if there was no other world than this. Somehow I hoped that the stairs would never end.

Reality struck again when we entered the cafe. Next to the large windows were two people, a man and a woman. I could not see their faces because of the backlight, but when we came closer I recognised one face. The lady from the restaurant, Agnes!

"Nice to meet you again!" she said, and gave me a warm hand. On the other side of the table was Edward, or "Eddie" as his friends usually call him, he said. Eddie seemed like a friendly guy, natty, somewhat guarded, surreptitious came to mind. Maybe he was a policeman? After I sat down next to Agnes she explained that we had met purely by accident, but when I went inside she felt something she wanted to follow up. She did that often she said, after all "in Amsterdam nobody really looks up from friendliness," she laughed again.

"And what do you think of the Sentinel?" Eddie asked. "Françoise already told us how you two met, oh, and we just learned you've also met Agnes already, briefly."

I thought for a moment. "Well, when I met Françoise I didn't know this would come out of it, and surely not when she had slipped her invitation into my camera. She's quite persuasive you know," I said, smiling, while Françoise smiled back at me.

"And so are you," she said and she put her hand on mine. For a moment I hesitated if I should pull back my hand, but I didn't. Instead Françoise squeezed my hand a little bit. The feeling I had on the staircase came back. My pause seemed a little bit too long, so now Agnes asked: "So, what do you think of the Sentinel?"

"I don't know. I don't even know what it is, I mean what she is?" I paused again. "I think I have to let this sink in for a while, maybe you can tell me more about what you know, why this had to be today, here and now?"

The waiter came with tea and *speculaas* cookies. After she had poured out tea for us Françoise started to explain some more.

"We think that by now about ten percent of the world population has seen a manifestation of a Sentinel. Like I said before, we call them Sentinels, but there are many other names being used. I like the "foo fighters", the way they have been described and reported by pilots from all sides of the Second World War, all thinking they were secret new weapons from the enemy. But there are also these reports that are far older of similar objects, like in the year 852 in Lyon, 1561 and 1566 in Nuremberg and Basel, and 1661 and 1667 in Berkshire and Mittelfischach. But there were many more, differently reliable but nevertheless. The ones that are seen in recent years seem to be more consistent, like round, opaque light balls, with a small range of colours, from white to orange or somewhat green."

I used her small pause to respond. "That's not what I saw. At first it was just a light, when it came closer I saw an opaque light ball indeed, but after it had stopped it became transparent, and I could clearly see an inner light structure, like an apple core," and I painted its shape in the air.

Françoise, Eddie and Agnes were frozen for a moment, then looked at each other and me again.

"That's remarkable," said Eddie.

"Amazing!" said Agnes.

Françoise was silent, I waited for her response.

"I, I'm amazed," she said, while leaning back, looking at me carefully, "you're saying she changed from an opaque light ball to a transparent, light form?"

"Yes, she did," I said, with emphasis on the "she", like Françoise had put it.

"We knew she'd be here today," Agnes said, "but I think she knew you'd be here today. And gave you a special welcome!" Agnes smiled, and Françoise nodded.

"Welcome, to the machine...," Eddie softly sang.

I looked at Eddie, and we both laughed out loud. Apart from that somewhat funny moment it seemed we all felt a bit awkward, all for different reasons I guess.

Then Eddie asked how my trip had been, and if I had come by train or by plane.

"By car," I said, "Maybe not the best choice, but it was a pleasant drive nevertheless." Wait a minute, I thought. How does he know I'd come by plane or train? Ah yes, Versailles. Did Françoise tell them everything?

After a while the atmosphere became more relaxed and Agnes suggested to have dinner together, as dinnertime actually was getting close, she said. Because most restaurants would have been reserved by now, she knew a good restaurant close by where she'd had lunch before. And as it was just outside the main tourist routes, she expected there to be room for us. We all agreed and out we went.

Outside Felix Meritis I turned to the left, but Agnes said:

"No, this way. Not the Leliegracht, we're going there, to the Huidenstraat."

It was even closer by than the Leliegracht so that was a relief. We passed a coffeeshop, and there was the restaurant.

This time Agnes and I had chosen the same menu, and we all had a kombucha as an aperitif. Somehow I had hoped Françoise had chosen the same as me, but then I also felt I shouldn't think like that. After we had almost finished our dinner Agnes said she wasn't feeling very well, but it wasn't too bad, she said. Ten minutes later she said she'd go home to her daughter's house close by, just a few minutes away. Eddie offered to bring her to the door and after a few hugs and kind words Françoise and I were alone.

"Shall we have a walk along the canal?" Françoise suggested as if she was reading my mind. I helped her into her coat, and out we went. It was dark, surprisingly mild, and quiet. We walked side-by-side, slowly, both thinking. Then, without saying anything Françoise looked at me and put her arm around mine and soon we walked as if we were walking in a different time, endless, warm, while I could feel my heart beating and my head gently spinning. It seemed as if the magical staircase was back.

Especially in the dark, it was easy to imagine we'd be walking there in another time. The street lights showing the warm colours of bricks, on the houses, on the pavement. It reminded me of a time when there were no worries, just joy. Excitement, adventure, exploration, wonder... joy.

"How are you feeling?"

"Good, thank you. And you?"

We both smiled.

"Great!"

We kept walking, holding each other's arms. Sometimes looking up to the canal houses and watching our steps on the *kinderkopjes*. Behind the facades was a mixture of darkness, late-working bureaucrats and domestic warmth.

"What do you think of these houses?" I asked Françoise when I remembered she studied art history.

"I think they all have wonderful stories of life. Good and bad, now and then. The Amsterdam Museum has some great reflections on them, have you been there?"

"Yes, several years ago, but I don't remember something in particular related to these houses."

Françoise pointed towards a house with elaborate carved ornamentation.

"What is a facade?" she said. "It is a layer in front of

something behind it. Is this layer hiding something? Is it an extension of what is behind it? Is it part of what is behind it, or is it separate from what is behind it?"

"You make it sound like it's a human being," I said smiling.

"Well of course," Françoise said, waving her hair around, and looking me straight in the eyes. "They are expressions of humans, good and bad, fake and real. But mostly fake, *helas*."

We walked further, and I took a closer look at the houses. And I took a closer look at Françoise. She noticed, turned towards me and suddenly kissed me on my lips.

"There you are, I wanted to do that the moment we went outside!" she said with the biggest smile ever.

"I'm glad you did."

Françoise did a step towards me, almost touching my chest, then moved up her chin, we kissed and I felt my whole body changing, like a wave and ripples passing through, as if I was shifting between different states of reality.

"She was here. Did you see her?" Françoise asked, still breathing full of excitement. "She just was here. I can feel it! Do you feel it?"

She slowly pushed herself against me, to share her excitement, or to feel mine? I felt confused, and very warm. Too warm, and I tried to open my coat. Instead Françoise took over and came into my coat. I could feel her body, her breasts, her nipples, her stomach and legs against me and wondered if my own excitement was getting too much.

I think she also noticed when she said "I think I have to go now," confirming there was more going on now than I thought there was, or something like that. We agreed to meet for lunch the next day.

After I had called my wife and we talked about what happened that day, well most of it, I went to bed, but hardly could get to sleep.

When I woke up the next day it seemed as if everything looked different. Was it that I felt different? Was it that I was different? Was it that the world was different?

I spent the morning at the Amsterdam Museum and the Schuttersgallerij. I enjoyed the large paintings, and thought of them as the facades Françoise was referring to. A layer, a cover story in front of the real story, or symbolising the real story, or just the story, not more, not less? Nah, they always were telling more than what they seemed to be. The displayed old colonial history was a black page, not just for the Netherlands, but for all colonial countries, and as such covered up by corrupt bureaucrats for generations, and ignored by those who preferred to see their national history only with rose tinted glasses. Times had changed.

For lunch Françoise and I met in a small restaurant close to her apartment. She told a little more about herself, how she lived most of the year in Amsterdam, as Brussels was only to complete her PhD, which she explained was about facades...

After our lunch was served we raised our glasses, and just when I was to say *proost*, Françoise said it was her birthday. Totally surprised I changed my words to wish her good health and joy, with a kiss, of course.

"I'm having a party tonight, with my friends. Would you like to come?"

"No, no, I'd love to come, but I'm supposed to drive back home this afternoon."

"Aah, really? Please?" she asked while holding my hand.

"Yes, really. I'm very sorry."

I felt awkward, as it seemed to make a big deal for her.

But I also had promised my wife to be back this evening, and had other obligations in the morning.

"Ah well, I can't have it all then," she concluded while getting the mood back up.

"Aries," I said, to open up the conversation again.

"Yes, she said, "but not that I know how I'm supposed to behave as such,"

"Me neither."

A little pause followed.

"Don't feel sorry," she said. "We can still do that another time. I hope your meeting with the Sentinel was worth it. I think it worked out, she came to see you, and showed you more than I expected."

"Oh, for me, I don't know. I don't know what to think, I don't know what to feel. I need some time to make up my mind about this. But we'll keep in touch, I think we may indeed have a lot more to talk about."

"Yes we have," she said gently but also with a somewhat serious smile.

"OK, I think it's time for me to hit the road again." With a kiss for her birthday and a long hug we said goodbye. I felt more emotional than I expected to be, but moved on. I checked out from the hotel, picked up my bag, and walked towards the parking garage. I took the lift to the third floor, the doors opened and I walked to my car... But I did not see my car where I expected it to be. Was I on the right floor? Yes I was. "Where is my car?!"

I walked up to the spot where I thought I parked it and looked around. Nothing to see. I walked back to the lobby and explained the situation, showed the prepaid ticket, my car keys...

At the police station it took half an hour before someone would get to my case. I already had called my wife to explain I would not be back before the evening as it seemed my car was missing. From the police station we went back to the hotel where the security manager had checked the security cameras' footage.

"Your car has been stolen," he said, and showed me the footage. "They came for your car," he explained. "They knew exactly what they had to do, see?"

I carefully looked what happened and I felt my anger rising. "Stop, go back a few seconds," I said. "That guy! That guy came up to my car a few days ago!"

The security manager zoomed in on the guy that had turned his face in the direction of the security camera and I clearly saw the man that had come up to my car to have a chat.

"He came to my car, looked at the interior and said how he had never seen this version before. He seemed to know a lot about it, like an enthusiast."

"An enthusiast alright," said the police officer. "Most probably he left a transmitter on your car, so they could easily find you, I mean your car."

I was dumbfounded, this could not happen to me!

"You see, they already took the car the same night you had parked it. Switching the number plates, *presto,* to the new owner in Eastern Europe, or just sold in parts."

I could not believe what I just heard. My dear 4C in parts...

When I was about to leave the security room I realised one more thing and asked to see the footage again. We all looked at the screen.

"Yes, those number plates. Those number plates! They drove past me, in my car!"

By now the hotel manager had also joined us and offered to have a drink in the bar, while he would check for some arrangements to be made. I had a talk with my insurance company, and another talk with my wife, the hotel manager said I could stay in the hotel for free tonight, before I could catch a train back home. Dinner was on him too... I wasn't hungry but was pleased with the gesture.

After I changed my mind and decided to take a few bites at the restaurant, I decided to give Françoise a call, after all I was to spend the night in Amsterdam again. She felt awful, as if it was all her fault. She said she was very, very sorry this had happened, and to "please come over..."

Seven

After they walk into the shop Chisato suddenly stops, turns around, and walks back out. Her father is nowhere to be seen.

"Wait here," she says. She walks back twenty, fifty metres. Around the corner, in the late evening shadow she sees her father sitting on a bench in front of a dark house. With his legs spread, he sits leaning forward and slowly turns his head towards Chisato. He looks worried, maybe in pain.

"I feel sick," he says. "I had to sit down for a moment," while stroking his stomach. "Maybe it's food poisoning."

Marie-Isobelle is standing in the door opening, looking for Chisato and her father. After a minute or two they appear from around the corner.

"He feels ill," Chisato calls out, "he just wants to lie down." Marie-Isobelle walks towards them, and together they bring him upstairs where he can lie down on a bed. They decide to do the tour of the shop on another day.

In her apartment, the next day, Marie-Isobelle looks outside the window. She looks down at the people, their colours, their brilliance, and thinks about her conversation with professor Kodaira. She looks at warm colours, the different colours of different people, the different colours of the houses, the water, the pavement. Did she just change the mood and the colours? Or did she change her own awareness of colours? How could she know she was a super-human? She walks away from the window, and runs back to see if there is a difference.

The telephone rings. It's Chisato.

"My father has died."

Marie-Isobelle is nailed to the ground. Her eyes wide open, her mouth open, but no sound.

"My father is dead," Chisato says again.

"I'm so sorry!" Marie-Isobelle finally responds. "Where are you? I'll come to you now."

The front door is open, but nobody is in the shop. She hears people talking upstairs and walks towards the stairs. Chisato comes down. They fall into each other's arms. A man comes down the stairs.

"Hello," he says, "I'm Chisato's uncle, her aunt is up-stairs with the doctor, and her father. Nice to meet you."

Chisato stays in Marie-Isobelle's arms.

His death wasn't totally unexpected, Marie-Isobelle learns at the funeral. In the last few years it seemed he didn't digest modern food very well, Chisato's aunt explains. Actually, western food always had been a bit of an issue, but he always tried to adapt, the kind and caring person he was.

Next to Chisato is a young Japanese man, but Chisato pays no attention to him, it's more like she turns away from him. There's little family, most people seem to be from some kind of scientific community, as they look serious and smart, Marie-Isobelle thinks. Chisato steps up to the little podium. Her words sound like a symphony, a bitter sweet symphony. There's no applause afterwards. There is no deeper black than the black of a funeral. There is no bigger contrast than with the living flowers, the colourful, living flowers, that soon, will die too.

Marie-Isobelle looks at the faces, one by one, as they walk away. She notices the different expressions and enhances them with mood colours. Nobody notices. Chisato does. She begins to smile, and barely can keep her laughter inside, but quickly recomposes. Before anybody notices.

"My father would have loved to see that," she whispers. They both smile with tears in their eyes.

During the next few days Chisato and Marie-Isobelle

spend a lot of time together, especially in the evenings, under the gentle, warm summer sky. Somehow there's a lot of comfort under trees, along canals, in small courtyards. Somehow Chisato and Marie-Isobelle are becoming friends, real friends.

"My father and I used to talk often about colours, moods, feelings and awareness, and his research," Chisato explains to Marie-Isobelle. "He loved to watch you, how you respond to the world. How the world responds to you. I think he also was a little bit in love with you." They look each other straight in the eyes and squeeze each other's hands, almost till it hurt. Tears flow again.

"It's OK," Marie-Isobelle softly says. "It's OK." Chisato kisses Marie-Isobelle on her lips, gentle, and passionate, then moves back, while looking each other straight in the eyes again. "It's OK," Marie-Isobelle says again. Then they fall into each other's arms as if it's for ever. It's for ever, no doubt about it.

It's weekend! Marie-Isobelle travels back home. She invited Chisato to come with her after she discussed it with us, but Chisato felt she'd better stay with her aunt and uncle. For Marie-Isobelle it's an opportunity to catch up with her astrophysics summer research project, for as far she can focus on it, so we give her as much space as possible, we even make it for her.

Françoise notices it first and makes me see; the colours had changed. Not just changed, but changed differently. Deep, very deep, as if they have another dimension, intense, as if they could just burst open. In waves, sometimes almost too much, like coming out of the surf and an even bigger one hits you.

"Something is going on, something is different," I say to Françoise.

"I don't know," says Françoise, "this is new to me!"

Françoise always had been a superhuman, from birth. If someone knows, she knows, I'm thinking. I feel confused, the colours are going from dull to bright, and beyond. And back. Then it starts to slow down.

Eight

While I was waiting in the colossal hall Françoise came walking towards me. I felt nervous, like an adolescent going on his first date, I felt comfortable, like a man visiting a lifelong friend. Françoise looked stunning, bright, radiating, as elegant and casual as only she could be. She had coloured her hair, deep orange. Her walk was like a dance in slow motion. But then again, every step was upbeat. Her hair was braided over her shoulder, like a thick ship's cable, her make-up dark and warm. I realised I had not noticed before that she was wearing make up at all. For a moment I actually wondered if she was the same person at all!

I presented the flowers that I had bought along the way. Plenty of flower shops in Amsterdam! Françoise closed her eyes as if she was going to dive into the flowers.

"*Délicieux!*"

Now I knew it was her, her eyes and her voice...

With her right hand holding the flowers, and her left hand holding mine, I followed her along the hallway. I almost stumbled, but corrected immediately. She turned her head for a moment, "Follow me," she said smiling.

We climbed a staircase and arrived at the front door of her apartment.

"Please, come on in," and I followed her inside. It seemed huge and the first impression only became larger with every following second. It was unlike anything I had seen before in Amsterdam. The timber floors seemed like ages old, solid and dark, the walls bright and minimalistic. I loved it already.

We moved from the bedroom floor to the main floor: an open space with exposed beams, living room, kitchen, ...and the other people I already heard on the lower floor, with some gentle music.

"Hi, hi, hi, hello..." I think there were some ten, twelve people and Françoise introduced each one of them, and me. There was only one familiar face: Eddie.

It looked like they had dinner together, as the kitchen had been occupied with empty bowls and some leftovers. In the background I heard familiar music, I think it was Radiohead. I was happy with Françoise's taste for music. Eddie waved, to make me sit with him, and as he made room I gladly accepted the invitation. While sitting down the room seemed even more spacey and I noticed the little floors on each side of the room, or roof space. Eddie started talking but I didn't hear him immediately. Some of the others seemed to study me, I felt a little bit like the odd one out, but then again, all seemed OK.

Eddie was talking to me "...You know Françoise and I go way back, don't you?"

"Ehm, no I don't. How so?" I wondered why he was telling me this. Then I noticed his eyes were saying that he might be a bit drunk, already?

I waited for Eddie to continue.

"He always says that," I heard Françoise's voice saying. She had brought a glass with something that looked like champagne. We toasted to her health, a happy birthday and a wonderful life. That should do it! After we all sat down again the music got louder and a few of the girls got up to dance, and I watched one of them dancing unbelievably beautifully, gracefully, on her own. I think her name started with an L, or was it Elle? Yes, it was Elle. Like a moving statue out of a painting by Jean Léon Gérôme...

Françoise had walked up to me slightly from behind and softly said in my ear: "Would you like to dance?"

"Of course!" How could I resist such an invitation! We danced, and we danced, and while the music was all around us, it seemed we were in a different space, and I noticed

Françoise dancing as beautifully and enchantingly like Elle. It seemed though as if with her everything became more colourful, deep, and amazingly colourful...

Then Eddie came piercing into our little bubble, he asked if he could dance with us... Of course we let him in, after all it was a happy birthday party. After a little while I felt an unpleasant tension, so I left the "dance floor".

I sat down on one of the sofas. Right in front of me was Elle. She looked me straight in the eyes, and raised her glass. I think she saw what was going on?

She then stood up, and came to sit next to me.

"Anything she can do, I can do better. Anything I can do she can do better," she whispered.

I turned my head towards her, and looked at her with amazement. Of course she was aware of the effect she had just caused and laughed, first a just a smile, and then a laugh. As if it was a joke. But it wasn't.

Elle raised her glass and asked if I also wanted one. She clearly felt at home in Françoise's apartment. After she came back with two full glasses of red wine we toasted on Françoise and "eternal youth". I don't know where exactly that came from, but we did. Her eternal youth I guess?

We talked about the deep orange-red colour of the wine and held it against the light. Then I noticed her hair colour was exactly like Françoise's... Elle had been an art student, but had dropped out she said. It wasn't entirely clear what she did now, but before we could explore that she started talking about the Sentinel. She knew about it. First it seemed that for her it was just a Sentinel, or Sentinels, as if she knew about several of them and they would all be the same.

"Françoise said you had seen it uncovered, naked?"

"Hm, naked," I repeated, "I hadn't looked at it that way." I paused for a moment. "Yeah, you may be right, maybe indeed she was showing herself naked!" Still thinking about what that would mean I took a sip from the wine.

"What did you feel when she did that?"

I noticed she also referred to the Sentinel now as "she".

"Did it arouse you?"

I wasn't prepared for that question.

"No it didn't, though later I realised it was quite an intense, impressive experience," I tried to explain.

"It would be about ten years ago," Elle said, "that Françoise and I had our first meeting together, with the Sentinel. Like they say, you'll never forget the first time!"

We laughed, and I noticed Françoise turning her head towards us. Still a happy dancer it seemed. More people seemed to be dancing now. I felt comfortable in my seat though, as it seemed Elle did. Maybe she liked to dance more when she had more space around her?

"Shall we dance?" she then suddenly asked. And again I couldn't say no, of course.

"You know Sentinels dance too?" she said in my ear.

I was surprised by her remark, but then immediately was distracted by the way she danced, introverted and extraverted at the same time, small and lively, elegant and clear. For a moment I thought I'd just stand still on the side and watch her, but then again, maybe also because I could feel the red wine was messing with my head. Not much, but it clearly was there. After a little while I thought the wine was getting to Elle too as she started to dance less composedly, more freely, mesmerising... I started to get hooked by her little nose piercing and felt a little bit annoyed as it was distracting me from Elle's beautiful dance. The little diamond kept glittering and I tried to ignore it. So it pulled my attention even more and I had to laugh about myself and then I noticed it didn't bother me anymore, even started to like it and I just enjoyed the ride.

"What did you think of the naked Sentinel?" she then asked again.

Once more she had caught me by surprise, and I answered with a simple "Yes, well ehm, yes." I didn't really know what to say, so I didn't say anything more.

"She likes you, doesn't she?"

"Well I guess so, I don't know," I responded with a smile.

"But you like her, don't you?" Elle said, while turning her eyes and head slightly towards Françoise. "Otherwise you wouldn't be here?"

I wasn't sure how to respond to that question, then she said, "I know what Françoise thinks and feels, and she knows the same about me".

"So you're very good friends then, when you share that much with each other?"

"It's not always been that way, but now I think that's just the way these things go," Elle said. "I think it's fair for you to know," she continued in my ear as the music was starting to make the conversation a bit harder.

At that point I looked around me and noticed everybody was dancing, even the odd couple that had been sitting away in the corner all the time. It seemed Françoise's apartment was wired for parties, literally and figuratively. The party lights were hidden behind beams and the sound system looked like just an ordinary, but stylish sound system. Stylish, like everything I saw from the apartment, like everything I saw from Françoise. I thought of her naked...

"I can see why she likes you," Elle then said. "I'll have another wine, can I get you one too?"

"Sure, thank you," I replied, as I liked a little pause too.

I walked towards one of the windows to have a look at Amsterdam's canals at night from above. I liked the lights being reflected in the water, they made me think about the stroll along the canals I had with Françoise. I thought about what had brought me here, Paris, Versailles, Françoise, my stolen car. And then I thought about calling my wife. Just when I was about to reach for my phone Françoise stood next to me with two glasses of red wine.

"Cheers," she said, "with the compliments of Elle!"

"Cheers, *santé!*" I replied and looked at Elle, who also raised her glass on the other side of the room.

Françoise put her hand on my back and came forward to give me a kiss. "Thank you for being here tonight. How are you doing now?"

"Mixed feelings," I said. At the moment I said that I noticed a reflection in the water moving and looked up.

Almost at the same height as the floor we were a light orb was hovering over the canal. Just a light orb, opaque white.

"There it is," I said, and pointed outside.

"Yoohoo!" Françoise said out loud. "Welcome to my party!"

Others noticed it too, inside the room, and outside along the canal. Soon we were all standing in front of the windows, but just as soon the Sentinel hovered away again. The only one I didn't see was Elle. She was outside on the small deck on the roof and came back in, she looked very happy, clearly amused as she came down the stairs. Françoise and Elle looked each other straight in the eyes, just smiled and threw kisses through the air. Françoise noticed me watching them.

"Yes, it's her party too, she's like my twin sister," she seemed to explain.

"I noticed," I replied. "*Santé* to the both of you then!"

"*Santé!*"

And we both emptied our glasses.

"*Santé!*" I heard behind me, and there was Elle with a bottle of wine in her hand, ready to refill our glasses.

"*Santé!*"

"*Santé!*"

"Santé!"

Soon the room filled with more people as more friends of Françoise and Elle had found their way up to Françoise's apartment. One year they'd celebrate in Françoise's apartment, the other year in Elle's, Françoise explained. It seemed like a cosy arrangement to me. Were they really twins? They didn't look like each other, both looking very beautiful, in their own way, they both seemed pretty smart too, but... hmm, they acted like twins alright. The way they seemed to be connected. I looked at Françoise again, without saying anything, and she looked back, without saying anything, at least not with words... The music would have made it hard to hear anyway.

After midnight, or more like about one o'clock, the first people started to leave, and the music became softer, the conversations louder. Still pretty well behaved. I was getting involved in more conversations with more people and while on the one hand I wasn't asked anymore who I was, or what I did, on the other hand I felt like I was accepted as one of the friends, not the odd one out anymore. I heard more stories about the Sentinel and more surprised responses about my meeting with the Sentinel and seeing her naked, as they continuously referred to the event. The others seemed both surprised and at peace with the whole happening. Soon everyone was talking about the Sentinel, I thought. I looked around in the room and noticed a painting that I decided to have a closer look at. For a moment it seemed as if it was the Sentinel, but when I came closer it looked more like the sun setting in the desert. I quite liked its unusual colours.

"It's Mars," I heard from behind me, "it's a sunset on Mars. The painting is called *Shifted*." I turned around and saw Elle standing behind me. We then had a pleasant conversation about the painting, about colours. Especially pleasant because it wasn't about the Sentinel.

It was somewhere between two and three when I was alone with Françoise and Elle. We started to clean up the place and Elle said, "I'll have a last glass of wine". Françoise and I agreed to also have a last one. While Elle came with three glasses in her hands, she stumbled a little bit, enough though to spill some of the wine over me. Spilled wine. It seemed unreal, it had actually never happened to me.

Françoise directed me to the bathrooms downstairs, next to the bedrooms.

I went down and looked for the bathroom but ended up in the bedroom, that had an ensuite bathroom.

While I started taking off my shirt I heard a knock on the door. Assuming it was Françoise, I said "Come in", it was Elle.

"I'm so sorry," she said. "Are you OK?"

"Sure, thank you, no worries," I replied, and continued with my shirt.

"You can have a look in that closet. I think she has a few shirts there that will suit you," she explained.

Then she took off her shirt.

"It's OK," she said, "Françoise knows."

Nine

Marie-Isobelle comes in. She looks calm, at ease. She walks towards the kitchen.

"Shall I make tea for us?" she asks.

"Yes please," Françoise says.

Indeed the colours are calmer now and I'm wondering what caused it. Is it my perception or are they really calmer?

"You know," Marie-Isobelle continues a little later, "I've forgotten to bring my personal laptop, and all my material is on it. So I think I'll have to go back sooner, tonight or tomorrow, sorry."

And so it is that our day begins with a disappointment, I was looking forward to sharing the day together.

"No worries," I say. "I'll get you to the airport. You can take the late airplane, that's cheaper, and come back tomorrow?"

Marie-Isobelle smiles. "OK, maybe I'll take the plane back the day after then."

Marie-Isobelle comes to sit with us, with the tea. All the terrace doors are open. Birds are talking, all kinds of different, gentle sounds. In the distance I hear a chainsaw, it's getting further away every few minutes. A few birds get louder. The weather is gorgeous and very calm. I see a tramper walking past. I imagine it getting too hot for a hike already. Argh, now the sound of a wood chipper is ruining the sounds of the birds. Luckily after a few minutes that's over. To be continued by the chainsaw. It's ruining my peaceful moment with my family, and while I try not to show my frustration, I see Marie-Isobelle is picking up on it. She puts her cup of tea down, and turns towards where the sounds are coming from. As if she's isolated a circle, a spot in the scenery, the colours vibrate wildly. Did she do that?

"Are you doing that?" I ask her. Françoise sits back and watches carefully.

"I think I might be doing that," Marie-Isobelle answers. "It's something I talked about with professor Koda. He made me aware I might be able to do that."

"To do exactly what?" I asked.

"To change colours. To change the colours of something, anything."

Françoise looks at Marie-Isobelle with her eyes wide open, she doesn't say a word, while Marie-Isobelle continues.

"Maybe it's something else, I don't know."

The machine noises have stopped, birds are chirping happily.

Françoise raises up from her chair and takes a few steps towards Marie-Isobelle and embraces her.

"Wow, I've heard about it, and you can do it, wow, I'm impressed, I'm so proud of you!"

"What in God's name are you talking about?" I ask with a somewhat raised voice.

Françoise and Marie-Isobelle turn their heads towards me, somewhat shocked.

"It's OK," Françoise says. "I'll explain darling."

After some fifteen, twenty minutes I feel like it's enough, for the moment. I heard things I never knew about my wife, and I see that Marie-Isobelle is in awe too. I feel it puts our entire relationship in a different perspective, and I'm not sure what it all means.

"So you've always known that it was not just about colours, and awareness," I try to summarise, "and that it's not just a passive thing either." Suddenly I feel a sense of calm and love come over me. I see Marie-Isobelle with a huge smile on her face. Françoise starts to laugh out loud, and Marie-Isobelle follows, I somewhat join in, not exactly sure why... I'm happy with them, that's why. Or is it Marie-Isobelle, changing the mood colours? Now I start to laugh out loud too.

"Oh dear, what does this all mean?" I ask the sky... Just when I think I'm coming to grips with changing colours, it seems the next level is dumped upon me, and I'm the last one to understand what is going on.

"I've tried to see how it works, how I can control it, how it makes people feel, how it changes things," Marie-Isobelle says. "Sometimes, a little bit, not too much, just trying to see how it works, like professor Kodaira told me. Trying to get a feel for it, trying to get a feel with it."

All the while Françoise just listens, with a smile on her face. A caring, loving smile. Somehow I want to make love with her, right now. But quickly I come to my senses, as there are other issues to deal with. The colours are beautiful when I walk outside for a moment. It's hard to know what is my perception, my awareness or Marie-Isobelle's mood change... Françoise comes standing next me, and holds my arm. Then she turns towards me and starts kissing me, sweet and gentle.

After we had an early dinner Marie-Isobelle gets her bag in the car, and we head on to the airport. The summer evening throws some pretty colours around us, this time I don't think Marie-Isobelle has anything to do with it.

"I don't think *maman* wanted to keep you out of the loop," she says "I think she actually thought you'd know about it somehow too."

"That's sweet of you to say, but it's not a problem. Your mother and I are still learning about each other. We'll find a way, we always find a way."

"I know," Marie-Isobelle says. "I just want you to know I love you."

"It's a bit confusing," I say. "It's giving me a bit of a headache, but it will be OK."

Some thirty, forty minutes later we arrive at the airport. Marie-Isobelle gets out and I take her bag out of the car. A kiss and off she goes. I try to smile as I see the colours around her changing, but my headache keeps me from it. In the car I decide to sit for a minute, till a guard signals me to move on. I drive a little further to stop at a parking lot, my headache is annoying me and I try to focus it away. It helps a little bit, enough to decide to drive home. I see colours change, as if something is changing in me. Different. I drive home slowly as the changes are somewhat distracting. After I get home I park the car just in front of the house and get out, the front door is slightly open. When I walk to the front door it slowly opens further. Françoise is standing in the door opening, with a lovely smile in soft blue lingerie and something like a little cape from the same fabric. It's like super woman has landed. Super sexy woman has landed in my house...

"Come darling," she said, "Marie-Isobelle called me to say you'd have a terrible headache. Let's do something about that."

She takes my hand and slowly leads us to the bedroom. The terrace doors are still open and the evening light fills the room with a gentle orange-reddish colour.

"It's OK darling," she softly says. "Relax."

Ten - Eleven

Not a single word was to be spoken. Gently she pushed me on my back on the bed. The room was softly lit, she had draped a few thin veils over the lamp shades, mostly red, and there were a few candles along the wall. High enough, so I could still see some of them while I was laying on my back. She towered above me, on her knees, sitting with her thighs lightly on my upper legs. She wanted to be on top, to be in total control. She took off all our jewellery, my watch, my glasses, as if she wanted us to be absolutely clear, absolutely transparent, absolutely naked towards each other, for each other.

She shook her head backwards, and with her hands she spread her hair wide, wild and 'round, she was hovering over me and with the light coming from behind her she was like an overwhelmingly radiating star. Radiating, wild, and yet in control. She moved closer towards me and lightly, gently sat on my stomach, warm on warm, soft on soft. She bent forward so I could kiss and smell her sweet white small grapefruit-sized breasts. I was like under a spell, I loved it. From one to the other, from other to one. For a moment she moved a little closer down towards me, closer, closer, and then slowly but firmly slid back. And in a movement that felt timeless, and yet lasted just one or two seconds, I was inside her, completely inside her, and she was all around me, all over me, as if we had become one.

I saw colours around us that I didn't even know existed. It felt as if I was in a different world, a different reality. It blew my mind, it blew my reality, it blew me beyond anything I had known.

Twelve

When I woke up the next morning there was a sense of timelessness. A deeper sense, as if we had entered a different dimension, a different time, a different zone, a different world. Surely, I thought, the world would never be the same again. Warm red lingerie was neatly folded over the back of the chair. I heard the shower running and I noticed something unfamiliar. A few moments later Françoise came out of the shower, with a gentle smile on her face. I looked at her in the gentle morning light, she looked like a statue of art. And then I noticed that little tattoo, just like I had noticed on Elle's neck.

"*Bonjour*," she said.

"*Bonjour*," I said, "what is this? I remember last night, and Elle coming into the room..."

"It's OK," she said smiling, "it's all OK."

"I'm not sure," I replied," I was in the room with Elle, and now I am here in your bed? What is going on?"

Françoise came sitting on the bed, I noticed that little tattoo was an M in a square. M squared? She then turned, leaned towards me and looked me straight in the eyes.

"Elle and I share everything," she said. "Everything, I feel what she feels, and she feels what I feel. I sense what she senses, I know what she knows. It's all OK."

Then I saw the clock and realised my train was leaving in about half an hour. Totally messed up I quickly got dressed and headed towards the train station. I had no idea what was going on with Françoise, or even with myself.

In the train I freshened up a little bit, and had a little bit of a breakfast. Little by little I started to come to my senses. Little by little I started to realise that I was in a mess. Why? What happened? That night must have been the beginning of the end, or the end of the beginning?

At the train station my wife was waiting. She noticed my messy state, even though I tried to be well composed. I explained that I had overslept and had to hurry to catch the train... She tried to cheer me up, but I felt too awful to respond well.

It took me a few days to find myself again, and my wife. It felt like a distant dream, but then the phone calls with the police, the insurance company and the hotel made me realise it all happened for real. Something extraordinary, something beautiful and something awful had happened. All at the same time. And I couldn't explain it to my wife.

After a few days my bag arrived that the hotel had sent to my home, and again Françoise had managed to slip a message to me.

"Please call me. Kisses, Françoise."

I didn't call, I was too overwhelmed with what had happened and was afraid of what could follow. Instead I tried to pick up my work, and started to look for another car, maybe another 4C, if I could find one. I liked that distraction, and so did my wife.

The next few weeks seemed to stabilise my life. The hunt for a new car was indeed distracting, amusing and gave some direction.

Almost every day we talked about the Sentinel and I found more information about the phenomenon, mostly quite different from my experience though. Why was it different? I wasn't sure if it was a good dream or a bad dream. Why me?

It felt as if my life had changed completely while I tried to keep it as normal as possible. How do you keep something abnormal normal? Or was it abnormal at all? I found myself thinking about it a lot. I felt like being in a higher state of consciousness, a higher state of awareness. The world had changed, our world had changed. I saw more of its beauty, and more of its ugliness. At first I wasn't sure if it was a good thing or a bad thing, but slowly I came to realise how in fact it felt like a deeper realisation of truths, it felt like choosing what belonged to me, and what not. Because we talked about it almost every day, it kept us both levelled, connected, at ease, balanced.

It was more than a month after I had been in Amsterdam that I found a message on my phone: "Please call me. Kisses, Elle." The similarity with the message from Françoise several weeks earlier made me feel nervous. Though I thought about calling back it felt as if I couldn't handle the complexity, and decided to do nothing about it and just go on with my life. Meanwhile my life didn't just go on. Clearly something was changed, and clearly it affected not just my life, but also my wife's life, our lives, especially as it turned out that she got pregnant shortly after I had returned from Amsterdam. I had told her about the birthday party, even that I had slept in Françoise's apartment, it seemed like it didn't really matter. What seemed to matter was that she was pregnant, that we'd be parents. I was deeply impressed with her. We decided it was good for us to take a break and visit another European capital during the summer holidays, that wouldn't take long anymore. This time we decided to visit London.

Time flies by, even when you're not entirely having fun. Although it was fun seeing all those little changes.

The weather in London was fine, not too hot, and mostly dry. Our hotel was close to Paddington Station, a practical spot and a very pleasant hotel, I should say "a pleasant management", as it's always the people who make it work, not the building. Ah well, a good start is half the battle...

Piccadilly Circus, with lots of different people. Trafalgar Square, with no people at all, as it was closed off. We walked through the city, found some pleasant places for coffee or lunch, and noticed all those silly old security cameras. Were they still working? Along the river Thames we stopped to enjoy the view towards Big Ben.

While I was taking pictures, a voice beside me said:

"Nothing is what it seems." It was Eddie.

"Eddie!" I said quite surprised. "What are you doing here?"

"Oh, I was just in the neighbourhood." he replied.

I introduced Eddie to my wife, and we talked a little about the scenery along the Thames and how very little had changed here over time. A few more shiny high-rise bureaucratic castles maybe, but in essence there still was a very conservative, traditional feel. But when Joan had walked a little bit away from us, Eddie asked: "Is your wife pregnant? Congratulations!", and then suddenly said: "Did you know Françoise is also pregnant?"

I looked at him somewhat bewildered.

"No, I didn't, I'm quite surprised."

"Well, the thing is," he continued,"I think it's your child."

Nailed to the ground I didn't say anything.

"It doesn't really show yet, and she doesn't say anything about who's the father, but I think it's you. Elle and Françoise say they plan to raise the child together. Well, I thought you should know."

Then he turned to Joan. "It was nice meeting you, I hope you'll have a great time together here in London!"

For the rest of the day I kept wondering what that was all about, but by the time we went for dinner I had decided to put it beside me as a weird story "full of sound and fury, signifying nothing."

The next day we gave the National Gallery another try, if Trafalgar Square was open to the public again.

It was open, and filled with a lot of tourists. But something was different, and I did not see what. Inside the National Gallery I heard a security guard explaining about an issue on Trafalgar Square from the day before, but that nobody really knew what it was about, and the police weren't saying anything.

At first I was a bid shocked with the dark, dull, somewhat bureaucratic atmosphere at the entrance, hardly worthy of a National Gallery I thought, but then someone seemed to have switched on colour lighting and the space came to life.

After a while I started to realise the feeling that was bothering me, it was the sense of brutal colonialism still being present after so many years, even though the aspect of conservation also still has its merits. When walking from room to room there was a battle between the beauty of the art, and the ugliness of what much of it represents.

Then I realised that it was not just the National Gallery,

but also, or even more, the short meeting with Eddie from the day before. I needed to shut it off, before it would really ruin our little holiday.

Thirteen

It's the next morning and I wake up with a sense of timelessness. A deeper sense, as if we have entered a different dimension, a different time, a different zone, a different world. Somehow, I realise, the world will never be the same again. Greenish-blue lingerie is neatly hanging over the back of the chair. I hear the shower running and I notice something unfamiliar. A few moments later Françoise comes out of the shower, with a gentle smile on her face. I look at her in the morning light, she looks like a statue of art. And then I look at her little tattoo, the little squared M...

"*Bonjour*," she says.

"*Bonjour*," I say.

A gentle kiss, and then the telephone rings. Françoise answers it.

"*Bonjour*," she says.

"*Bonjour*," Marie-Isobelle says.

They both laugh, it's lovely to hear them laugh.

"It's so lovely to hear you mum. I already miss you."

"I miss you too darling," Françoise says, still standing in front of the window, the light encapsulating her enchanting contours. I think I'll have to tell her my headache came back...

"You know mum, I have to tell you something serious. In the news here in Amsterdam they said they are looking for someone they called Edward H., for the case of a deliberate food poisoning in Amsterdam, and then they showed the restaurant where we had dinner with Chisato and her dad."

Françoise sits down, I know I can forget about my headache now. I realise the situation and decide not to interfere, and listen to Françoise and Marie-Isobelle.

"Is everything alright with you?" Françoise asks.

"Yes, yes, sure mum. I already had planned to see Chisato while I'm here, so now I'll sure have to go and see how she's doing and if indeed it is related to her father's food poisoning. Maybe I'll stay one or two days longer."

"Of course, take your time, there's no hurry. And if you need anything, your father and I are here for you. Say hi to Chisato from us."

"I will mum. I love you both."

"And we both love you Mai. Bye darling."

"Bye parents."

Marie-Isobelle puts on a summer coat and goes outside.

She walks along the canal and tries to focus her mind. Everything seems to slow down, colours seem to come out of nowhere, and then... she lets go. Things seem normal again. Marie-Isobelle giggles.

When she arrives at Chisato's house, the shop is still closed. Chisato opens the door and is very surprised.

"What are you doing here?" she says, both enthusiastic and surprised.

"I came to pick up my laptop from my home that I had forgotten, and then I heard in the news something about food poisoning in the restaurant where we were with your father."

Chisato looks at Marie-Isobelle with her eyes wide open. Then she whispers, "I had a man visiting yesterday, he told me everything."

"What do you mean with everything?" Marie-isobelle asks with caring, frowning eyes.

"Come in," Chisato then says. They hug and walk in.

"He asked me if I had ever heard of Operation OK, or actually just OK, short for Operation Kodaira. Of course not I told him, but of course I wanted to know why it was called Kodaira. It was a huge story, sit down, and I'll make a tea."

"It's OK," Marie-Isobelle softly says, somewhat meditative even.

Chisato didn't notice. While she puts up a kettle and takes a few mugs from the cupboard she starts telling the story.

"OK stands for 'Operation K.', 'Operation Kodaira' and even is used as an inside joke the guy said. 'OK is KO' they say now."

"That sounds a bit cold," Marie-Isobelle says.

"Well yes, he wasn't the warmest kind of person, but he did seem concerned."

She pauses for a moment.

"They didn't do it, he said. The guy we should be looking for is Edouard Hubert, also known as Edoardo, Edward or Eddie, with changing surnames though. He's a dimensional time-traveller, of the sneakiest kind!"

"A what?" Marie-Isobelle replies.

"Oh, it gets more insane alright," Chisato continues. "He's a bad guy, the agent said."

"What agent? You didn't say he was an agent?"

"Some kind of agent, American, Australian, I'm not sure."

"But what about that dimensional time-traveller?"

"Well, when he first came to our time, or our dimension actually, he worked as a professional sneezer. They are strictly illegal now he said. They'd travel to international airports, where a lot of international travellers are closely together, and would sneeze, infect as many as possible travelers. It was to spread diseases for the multi-national pharmaceutical industry. They'd even go to ski resorts where rental ski boots would be infected with fungi."

Marie-Isobelle looks quite disturbed.

"Should I wait with the tea for a few minutes?" Chisato then asks.

"No, it's OK, I mean, it's alright."

Chisato pours out some tea.

"The guy said it is for my safety to know about him. Operation Kodaira was of international significance, he said, and a lot of bad people were after it, or actually are still after it."

The colours in the room start to fade and then become harsh and cold. Marie-Isobelle and Chisato are both quiet for a few moments and take a sip of tea. The colours in the room start to swirl, first slowly, then increasingly wild. Chisato and Marie-Isobelle both look at it, then it becomes calmer, more balanced, and after a deep sigh, it seems to become normal again. Warm, caringly normal.

"Would you like a cookie with that?" Chisato then asks.

"Yes please," Marie-Isobelle says laughing. "You make me think," she then continues, "that guy, was it really about your safety, or is that the usual trick to make you believe he was there for you?"

"That's a good point, he did ask quite a lot, but then again, if that poison Eddie is real, then I sure like to know about it. He said he moves through the fifth dimension, parallel dimensions, as a kind of 'self-projecting hologram' on a grey, ehm, adaptable body?"

"That's a mouth full, well you know, I've seen some unusual stuff already, so yeah, why not?" Marie-Isobelle responds.

"Oh well, you think that was all? Wait till you hear this: he doesn't travel into the future, he can only travel back from the future! He explained it like some kind of grey plasma. He doesn't move through dimensions through gravity, or love, he doesn't even know what love is, but through something else, which can only be labelled in our dimensions, but not explained. He acts, mimics human emotions, which is typical for someone, or something like him, to copy human behaviour, human emotions."

Marie-Isobelle listens quietly, trying to imagine what this all means.

"Isn't that what we already say about our politicians, our corporate leaders?" she says. "You know, that they only act like caring human beings, but in fact are more like predatory, cold-blooded, cold-hearted reptiles?"

"Hm..., when it's winter, then he would be slower, and easier to catch?" Chisato says laughing.

"You know, really, about that agent, why would he tell you all this?"

"I don't know," Chisato replies, and she stands up to reach for the teapot. While pouring out the tea, she expresses some concern: "He did ask a lot about my father, and what I know about his research."

"See, that's my issue, to me it looks like they all want to know about the colours, even though I think a lot is known already and the colours could just be a secondary, or even tertiary aspect of a different phenomenon that we are not yet aware about. Forgive me for saying it so bluntly, but why would they want to kill your father for that?"

"Oh, that's crossed my mind also..."

The rest of the morning they sip more tea, and talk small

stuff. The big stuff seems exhausting. After lunch they take a walk together along the Amsterdam canals. They listen to a street performer singing "Celtic New Year", even though that's still months away.

"Neopagan or fake neopagan?" Marie-Isobelle says jokingly, not too loud.

"I like his voice," Chisato says.

"I like his colours," Marie-Isobelle responds.

Chisato turns to Marie-Isobelle.

"Don't do it Mai!", Chisato says in a slight panic.

"No, of course not," Marie-Isobelle reassures her.

They continue their journey laughing.

Some shops are closing. The first bureaucrats are going home. It's dinnertime. They decide not to go to that restaurant anymore. After a little while they stand in front of an Italian restaurant, "*Ottimo*" it says.

"That's very good," Marie-Isobelle says. The restaurant owner sees and welcomes them.

"Nice to see you again," he says to Marie-Isobelle, "and very kind to bring a new friend to our restaurant."

"Wow, I didn't expect you to remember me, great memory."

"I remember beautiful customers," he replies with a kind smile. "I'm Giovanni, but some customers prefer to call me John, as you please."

He directs them to a table close to the entrance, cosy and still with a view outside. After they've studied the menu they both have chosen for the "spinach fettuccini, cherry tomato, roasted capsicum, garlic, mushrooms & flavoured crumbs", made with their homemade vegan pasta. Giovanni comes to take their order.

"We both would like the Spinach fettuccini please."

"And with a glass of *lambrusco* for both of us?" Chisato asks.

"I have a great *lambrusco dell'emilia* for you," he replies politely.

After dinner is served, the conversation goes back to where they left it in the morning.

"How do you feel about what happened, with that guy, you know, that agent?" Marie-Isobelle asks.

Chisato looks at Marie-Isobelle, and starts to cry. Marie-Isobelle puts down her fork and moves to the other side of the table. She puts an arm around Chisato.

"I'm so sorry," she says.

"Is there something wrong?" Giovanni asks.

"No, no, thank you, we're fine," Marie-Isobelle replies, both comforting Chisato and reassuring Giovanni.

While Marie-Isobelle tries to change the atmosphere, the colours change with it. It lifts Chisato's spirit. Even Giovanni seems to notice something, but that's not clear. It's probably not clear for Giovanni either.

They finish their dinner without emotional interruptions, but with lots of staring in each other's eyes. Lots of smiles too.

"Would you like a dessert?" Chisato asks Marie-Isobelle.

"Sure, if you like one," Marie-Isobelle replies.

"Did you enjoy your Spinach fettucini?" Giovanni comes asking.

They both confirm it was *ottimo*.

Giovanni smiles.

"Can I offer you *Un Gelato al Limon* on the house?"

"Yes please!"

Marie-Isobelle already starts licking her lips with her warm purple tongue.

Two days later Marie-Isobelle is home with her parents. She tells about Chisato's story, and the agent that came to her house. Françoise listens carefully, and starts to talk.

"I think he may also be an employee at the M-institute, but not the same department as me."

Both Marie-Isobelle and I focused our eyes on Françoise, very curious as what would follow.

"I've heard of Operation K., but there are so many projects that I don't know them all," she continues.

"In the early history of M, when it was still a small organisation, when the MOUs, 'Mild Organic Upgrades', were changed into MODUs, for 'Mild Organic DNA Upgrades', there was also a mention of Operation K., but it seemed it was a sidetrack that was not of real concern to my department, so I never really looked into it. I will have a look tomorrow at the office to see what I can find out."

"I'm sorry mum, but what are MODUs?"

Françoise pauses for a moment.

"I'm a MODU," she then says.

I knew, but Marie-Isobelle stares at her mother with her eyes wide open.

"When the world was starting to get swamped with cold AI robots, people started worrying about the future of mankind. Riots followed and eventually the number of cold robots declined, but the concept of Artificial Intelligence already had left its mark on humanity. That is when people looked for ways to increase the quality of the human brain, the quality of human thinking, the way humans used their brains, in a semi-natural way."

Françoise takes a deep breath.

"Yes, there have been lots of experiments with victims of wars, especially soldiers, but eventually they found a way, without cutting and pasting, that added a third basic struc- ture on top of the old brain, as an expansion of the corpus callosum."

Françoise points with her finger to the top of her head.

"People had slightly flatter heads back then."

Marie-Isobelle feels at her own head.

"Yes, it's hereditary."

In the evening we're all sitting comfortably in the living room, reading, writing, drinking tea, when Marie-Isobelle starts telling about the last evening in Amsterdam, yester- day, before she came back home. She tells us about some- thing quite amazing that she had seen; a hovering ball, a transparent, hovering ball with light-emitting wires, like an apple core.

"I was outside, close to my apartment, at a bridge on the Keizersgracht, when I looked up high between the canal buildings, and there it was. I heard someone say: '*Ç'est la Sentinelle'*."

Fourteen

A few months had passed since our little summer holiday to London. Time flies when you're having fun? I watched my wife becoming more pregnant by the day. She clearly enjoyed the changes of her body. Autumn had arrived in our neck of the woods. Sometimes I felt as if time was actually speeding up!

While we were still in London the news was filled with a strange issue that happened on Trafalgar Square, the actual reason that it was closed off: in the early hours on that specific morning when we first planned to visit the National Gallery there had been some kind of an explosion, but with no sound, more like a lightflash, without smoke or any damage. And even though it was small, as shown on TV from the security camera footage, there was a panic response and the search was on for a person that actually looked like Eddie. But they could not find him, not even his name.

I avoided thinking about Eddie, Françoise, Elle, Amsterdam for a while, but as always, what you avoid thinking about, you do think about. I started to feel guilty, even though I felt I tried to do the right thing. It all made sense, and it didn't make sense. It all felt good, and it didn't feel good. Time seemed to behave like waves, slow and fast, and sometimes totally quiet. Those were moments like sitting at a lake, with no wind, and all of its calmness comes to you, becomes part of you, and you become the lake. And the lake becomes you. Deep. Deep and wide, omnipresent, dark and light, colourful and colourless.

"Another tea, darling?"

I jumped back into the present.

"Yes please!"

Six months pregnant and still as vivid as a bird. She won't slow down, even though her body is clearly changing and gaining weight. It's more the balancing act I worried about though, literally and figuratively. Or was I projecting my own state of mind? A deep sigh.

"Would you like me to bring the tea?" I asked her.

"No, it's OK."

It was as if her being pregnant was bringing more colour to our lives, literally and figuratively. She noticed the smile on my face and blew a kiss through the air.

"I love you," she said.

"I love you too," I replied.

She was sitting relaxed, reading something, while I was just sitting, looking outside, watching the wind gently blowing through the trees, the leaves rolling in front of them. Suddenly I felt like drowning in this sea of kindness, and soon I realised something was nagging in my mind and it just would not stop. After a while I decided to give Françoise a call and went to my study, sat at my desk and found myself in doubt about calling Françoise, yes or no. I called her, but instead of Françoise I was talking to Elle.

"Hel-lo stranger!" she said.

"Oh, hi Elle," I replied.

"So, what brings you here?"

"I actually was trying to reach Françoise."

"Oh, I'm sorry, but she's not home today."

"I'm sorry for bothering you. And how are you doing?"

"Ah, we're doing just fine, great actually. Thank you for asking."

"Should I call back for Françoise tomorrow?"

"You sure can try."

"OK, thank you Elle! Bye!"

"Thank you darling, bye-bye."

I was both disappointed and glad that I had missed

Françoise. I clearly wasn't well prepared to talk to her. Elle, on the other hand, seemed to accept it as perfectly natural and just seemed to go with the flow. She felt warm and confusing. I needed a drink, but it was far too early in the day for me.

"It's all pretty dark matter," my wife said when I returned to the living room.

I was a bit surprised, shocked at her comment coming out of nowhere.

"What do you mean?" I asked.

"Your face, it's all over your face," she said smiling.

"I was just reading about dark matter," she continued, "and then you come in with that face!" Now she started laughing out loud and I started laughing with her.

"The things we learned," she said, "in the last twenty, thirty, fifty years, have shifted our realities, and changed our realities as such in such ways, that it's hard to imagine what people were thinking, say, fifty years ago. I mean, imagine your understanding of today's world if you would not have known anything about what they then called "dark matter" and "dark energy". Imagine where we'd be now? Pretty amazing, isn't it?"

I just listened in awe, stood up, and gave her a warm kiss.

"You're beautiful," I said.

"If indeed five-dimensional matter is structured all around us, then why don't we see it, is what this article asks. Can you imagine living in a world where such questions were asked, and yet there was no definite, no clear, no well-understood answer?"

"Well, if not for you, I may not have known either," I replied.

"Well yes," she said with a smile, "but it's also the other way. Let's have dinner, it's dinnertime."

Later that evening the phone rang. I picked it up, and before I said something I heard a voice saying: "Hi, it's Françoise, you had called?"

It was an automated voice, even though it was hard to tell the difference. A moment later I heard her real voice.

"Hi, how are you? Elle said you had called?"

"Yes, do you have a moment, I'll take it in my study."

As we already had finished our dinner it was easier for me to take the call in private, even though I thought that maybe I shouldn't.

"Sorry for the wait, thank you," I said.

"Sorry for disturbing you," Françoise replied, "how are

you?"

"Great, great, it's good to hear your voice. And how are you?"

"We're wonderful," she said, "yes I know, we had an argument with Eddie. I don't think he should have told you so bluntly."

"So it's true," I stated, both surprised and confirmed.

"Yes, Elle and I had decided to tell you, but at a later stage. We had decided to raise the baby together, and now would be a good time to tell. Please don't be mad at me, I do love you."

"I'm not mad at you," I said, "I'm somewhat confused. As if all I do nowadays is being confused. You and the baby are OK?"

"Yes, *merveilleuse*, we could not be better. Are you sitting down? Because while we're at it, we may just also tell you the rest of it. Elle is also pregnant."

It was as if my ears stopped hearing. I knew it, and yet I totally blocked it out. A deafening silence formed in my head.

It wasn't till I heard her say my name and ask if I was still there that I came back to the present. I was flabbergasted, totally out of this world. This was new, this was unheard of and it was mine. Or was it?

"Please don't worry," she said, "everything will be alright."

Although I did have faith in her I wasn't comfortable with the situation.

"I'll call you back tomorrow," I said.

"It's OK darling, good night!"

Fifteen

Somewhere, in what looks like a dark hotel room, with a small light on a desk, Eddie sits watching and listening. A screen shows a room, something like a study, and voices, saying: "I'll call you back tomorrow", "It's OK darling, good night!"

He makes notes. Then he stands up from the desk, switches off the screen, puts sunglasses on and walks towards the door. When he walks through the door, several people are walking behind it.

"Hi Françoise," he says.

"Hey Eddie, where have you been?" she asks.

"Oh, here and there, you know, the usual stuff. Check, check, double-check. Not very exciting, it's the perks of the job I guess."

They both go different ways. Françoise walks into a room in warm and light colours, it's her office. Bamboo timber dominates the atmosphere. In a display are several medical models of brains. On the wall are a few charts of nervous systems. She walks towards the window and takes in the views towards the mountain and after a deep sigh turns towards her desk with a colourful picture of her family, from when Marie-Isobelle was about five years old. The picture changes into a screen.

"Get me the current files, from this year, of the Sentinel," she commands. A larger screen appears with several files of texts and pictures.

"I thought so," she says to herself.

"Get me the files of Operation K., and the files of Edouard Hubert."

After reading for about half an hour she gives the command to find time parallels between the files and put them side-by-side.

"Add the older files from the Sentinel."

After another fifteen minutes there's a knock on the door. Françoise closes the screen and opens another one. A security manager comes in.

"How are you? We've had a warning that something in the system may be wrong. Is everything OK?"

"Everything's OK, thank you!"

And as quickly as he came in, he's gone again. Françoise decides to leave early, take the files home and study them there.

Later that afternoon, with a cup of tea, she starts to talk about what she'd found in those files.

"I've just seen a little bit," she explains, "but already I noticed parallels I didn't realise before."

She looks both worried and thoughtful. I don't interrupt as to not disturb her line of thought.

"Have you ever had the thought that you may not be who you think you are?"

Now she gets me worried.

"No darling, I don't think so. How so?"

"I found my name in an old file, that connects me to Operation K., Operation Kodaira, where all the superhumans started."

"Yes, well we know you're a superhuman. That's alright isn't it?"

"Yes, but I'm second generation, Mai is third generation. I think it looks like you and I did not meet by accident, we were chosen, selected, to have Marie-Isobelle, as our child. As our natural child."

It's quiet for a few moments.

"Marie-Isobelle is the first generation of naturally born superhumans, and we didn't have a clue! I think you and I were paired, to be studied. I didn't get the job because of what I had studied, but because so they could study us. Oh, I'm so sorry!"

Françoise hides her face behind her hands, while tears start rolling. I get up from my chair and kneel beside her, holding her.

"There's nothing to be sorry about, France. You're good, we're good. We'll have a better look at it together."

Françoise comes back up from behind her hands.

"Let's not yet tell Marie-Isobelle about this, not yet. We need to understand more."

I go to my study to give it some more thought, look up some things. A few minutes later, the door flings open.

"Hi dads, I'm back," Marie-Isobelle said.

"Hey sunshine! How was your little hike?"

She gives me a big hug, and I nearly fall over. We both laugh.

"I thought about the Sentinel that we talked about. Sometimes, when I'm walking in the woods I do feel as if there is something with me, hovering with me, and today I felt the same. So I tried to focus my mind on kind thoughts, warm, and turned my focus up into the top of the trees, and in that beam of warm colours a hovering ball lit up, I think it was the Sentinel indeed. And it beamed back, very kind and peaceful. Our beams formed into a ball which encapsulated us both. We stayed there for maybe a minute and then she gently moved away."

"You said 'she'?"

"Did I? She felt like a she alright."

"That sounds beautiful, Marie-Isobelle. Nothing else happened to you? Everything is OK?"

"Everything is OK dad, where is mum? I want to tell her."

"She just was in the living room."

We walk into the living room, but she is not there. Then our attention is drawn towards the garden, we see a large ball of colourful light, and Françoise is standing in the middle of it. We open the terrace doors and walk towards her.

"Come here," she says smiling.

I hesitate for a moment, but Marie-Isobelle runs towards her, and Françoise gives her a big hug. I couldn't be left behind, so I join in. From within the ball everything looks different, like a superimposed reality, an extra layer, extra depth. Intense, very intense. It gives me a headache.

"I have to get out," I say, holding my head, and step out.

"I waited for this moment to share with you," Françoise

says, "this was the right moment."

Meanwhile the ball slowly disappears.

"It's just growing pains darling," she continues, "growing pains, you'll be alright in a minute."

They both come to sit down with me on the lawn. Within a minute indeed I start to feel better.

"Wow, that was intense!"

Françoise looks us both in the eyes.

"We need to be strong, together, the three of us. I've looked up several files from our archives and found information that seems to concern the three of us."

"What files? What information?" Marie-Isobelle asks.

"I'm only just studying the files, Marie-Isobelle," Françoise answers, "we'll talk about that later."

I feel like a second-class human, both my wife and daughter superhumans, and me just an improved model. But, I realise, I'm catching up!

"What kind of files are you talking about, mum?"

"Oh, the files are from Operation Kodaira and the Sentinel you mentioned, and also from one of our secret agents, Edouard Hubert."

Marie-Isobelle jumps up.

"Edouard Hubert? That sounds like the name that agent

told Chisato!"

She pauses for a moment.

"The agent that visited Chisato said to look out for a guy named Edouard Hubert, a time-traveller, a bad guy."

Françoise listens and is thinking.

"We need to find out if we're talking about the same Edouard Hubert," Françoise says.

She projects a face of Edouard Hubert.

"I've only seen him on a screen, from a distance, but it could be him," Marie-Isobelle says.

"OK, more to add to the puzzle," I say, "let's get inside and I'll make us a tea, or is it dinnertime already?"

We decide to do both.

Sixteen

Time seemed to be slipping from right under me. It was as if a tiny black hole was pulling my reality away. My mechanical watch was running slow, so I went to my watchmaker who adjusted it. After a month my perfectly adjusted watch was running slow again. Then the watchmaker told about his other clients with mechanical watches; they all had the same issue, as if time was speeding up, without affecting mechanical watches. And to make matters worse, my headaches seemed to become more frequent; smaller, but more frequent, like tiny ripples on a lake. Growing pains, my wife said.

"Growing pains," Françoise said.

During the last month our contact seemed to become more frequent also, friendly, kind, as if we were both trying to make the best of a difficult situation. *La Sentinelle* was also back on the menu.

"As I'm in Brussels every two, three weeks, would you like me to come over for a visit while I'm there? Maybe I could also meet your wife?"

I liked the idea, but didn't want to decide alone.

"Wow, sure, but I'll have to ask my wife to see what she thinks of it."

Well, she said she likes the idea, actually that she'd be looking forward to meet the woman she'd heard about, but didn't have an idea of what she looked like. And after I had told she's also pregnant, she looked forward to it even more.

We looked over the lake; calm, small ripples, distant clouds, autumn colours, no headache. She took my hand, we smiled. Far away, someone was watching.

Eddie moved, the sphere dissolved, he took his bag, switched it off and hung it over his shoulders. He was in Amsterdam and knew exactly where to go.

Elle moved, the train left the station, she took her bag, and hung it over her shoulders. She also was back in Amsterdam and also knew exactly where to go. Though being pregnant slowed her down a bit. First a night's sleep.

The next morning there was a knock on the door. Elle answered it, and Eddie was exactly on time.

"Wow, look at you! Stunning! I still can't believe you

pulled it off like that. They seem to like you, since you're still here?!"

"Yeah, good morning to you too punk!"

A moment of silence, and then they both burst out in laughter.

"Ouch," she said, "it's too much!"

They both went inside where it was warm and cosy.

"Hot chocolate?"

"Yes please," Eddie answered.

"Françoise won't be here today," Elle said, "she has an appointment for a check-up. Agnes should be here any minute."

"You don't need a check-up?"

"I had mine yesterday. Everything's fine."

"Good, good."

Another knock on the door.

"I'll open it," Eddie said.

Agnes was standing with her coat over her arm.

"I'm exhausted," she said. "How those two do it, I have no idea."

"You must visit them more often," Eddie said, "you'll be as young as them in no time!"

Agnes laughed out loud.

After they all sat down with a cup of hot chocolate Eddie started to talk.

"We have competition," he said, "but we don't exactly know who they are. Not yet."

"How come we don't know?" Elle asked, while sipping from her hot chocolate.

"As I'm still not omniscient, I guess it's not someone I would know?" Agnes asked.

"Correct," Eddie answered with a smile, "but as I said, we don't know either, yet. Well, he may be something like another time-hopper, that's the least we think we know."

"And what is it they want?" Agnes asked.

"What it looks like at the moment," Eddie said, "it relates to Operation K., they may want to stop it, so, yes, it looks like they want to stop what we are trying to save for the future."

"Is this dangerous?" Agnes asked.

Eddie paused for a moment.

"I don't know, we don't know how far they're willing to go. So, yes, it could very well be dangerous. We need to be alert to say the least. We've already placed close protection on the young professor Kodaira and his research."

"And what about Françoise and me?" Elle asked.

"You two are well protected by each other, and me. He's just alone and as it seems for now he's working according to Earth protocol, he can not directly, ehm..."

"Kill...," Elle completed, "the ultimate intervention."

Then there was silence in the room.

"May I add one more thing," Agnes then said, "yesterday afternoon there was another security footage in the local crime news, and it looked again that you were in it Eddie. I think you may want to be more careful, or have it removed."

"What footage?" Eddie asked, while Elle looked anxiously surprised.

"A gang of what they labeled as organised East European car thieves, where you can be seen giving something that looks like an envelope to the old guy that they are now looking for. So now they're also looking for you, and they already had footage from you at the restaurant from a few months ago. I think they may think that you're a member of a gang, that gang," Agnes explained.

Seventeen

"We know that several weeks ago another traveller visited professor Kodaira's daughter Chisato. We know they've taken some of the research documents, and at least a list with names from his research. And we know that they know that we know now," Françoise further explains while we're preparing dinner together. She seems somewhat agitated.

Marie-Isobelle sits and listens. Colours are slightly changing.

"Don't do that now," Françoise says.

"What?" Marie-Isobelle replies.

"What?" I ask.

"I can feel it," Françoise says, slightly annoyed, but also slightly amused.

"I just tried to make you feel good," Marie-Isobelle responds, "I want to make you feel good and then the colours around you started to change. Things are changing, when I close my eyes, it seems like I can see the flows of energy in everything around me."

Françoise looks admiringly at her.

"It's growing on you," she replies.

"I close my eyes, only for a moment and the moment's gone," is the best I can think of.

Marie-Isobelle and Françoise both laugh, I look at them and feel nothing but love.

After dinner we try to see how well it works for Marie-Isobelle, or how it works at all.

Marie-Isobelle sits quietly, she focuses on her mood and the mood she wants to project. Françoise and I are the sitting ducks and let it come over us.

"OK," she says, "here comes."

"I feel bored," Françoise says, smiling.

"Don't do that, mum! I'm trying to be serious."

It looks as if her body is starting to glow, different colours gently pulsating, then it goes wider and the room lights up with her. I feel comfortable, but Françoise seems to feel more than just that. The light seems to concentrate around her, then suddenly it is as if it is encapsulating me too. Two colourful drops of light, growing smaller and smaller, as if the light enters our bodies, our minds.

I look at Marie-Isobelle, it seems as if she's in some kind of trance, with her eyes open. I feel gentleness, love.

Then both Françoise and me suddenly sit up straight,

alarmed, shocked, and we look at each other.

"Yes," says Marie-Isobelle, "I can do it, I can make you feel terrified!"

The colours seem to diminish, Marie-Isobelle relaxes a bit in her chair.

"It doesn't feel terrifying," Françoise says, "but I can see what you're trying to make me feel."

Then she startles.

"Oh, yes, that is terrifying alright, thank you, you may stop."

"For me it wasn't that strong, but indeed it became stronger," I added.

"I think I see what professor Kodaira was looking for," Françoise says, "and what Operation Kodaira was, or is about. I'll have to think about it."

Eddie climbs out of a window. He takes his communicator and calls Françoise.

"Hey Françoise, I think we need to have a talk soon, I mean now. Security is on to you, and me."

Half an hour later Eddie is at her house.

"I need to talk with you and your family," he says.

After they all sit down in the living room Eddie begins to talk.

"OK, I knew this would come, but not this soon. I noticed someone from Security is checking our files and they have noticed what you're looking for. Me. Well not just me, but the real me."

I look at Françoise, and the look in her eyes tells me she's thinking the same as I.

"Is this about Kodaira?" I ask Eddie.

"No, no..., well yes," he replies.

He takes a moment, while we all focus our eyes on him.

"Well, that's what it's all about," he then continues. "Oh, I didn't prepare this well enough. Where do I start?"

He takes another moment, this time he looks at all of us.

"I just came from my office, I actually fled from my office. Someone from security was about to come to my office, and that would have messed things up."

He sighs and sits slightly more comfortably.

"I am not who you think I am, and you are not who you think you are."

"I think we were about to find out, right?" Françoise says, "Or, we are about to find out?"

"Yes," Eddie replies.

"What I'm about to tell you is highly classified. You can talk about it with each other, with me, but with nobody else. It will be our secret. Our secret of existential importance."

He sits back, seemingly relaxed.

"OK, OK, OK..., you know what OK stands for, right? Operation Kodaira. Yes, it's where it all started. Or I should say, it's when it all started, but hardly where it ended, or ends. In the future the research, the findings by professor Kodaira will become essential for the continuity of human life on Earth. Yes, I'll say it as bluntly as it is. The power of the human mind is godly, no matter if you're a religious believer or not. Humankind will grow beyond whatever they've been told by their handlers, their controllers... Despite everything they've been told."

It's getting dark and a few lights switch on. Marie-Isobelle sits with both hands around her cup of tea. Françoise with her arms folded while leaning back into the cushions. And I, I could be a copy of her.

"I'm a dimensional time-traveller," he says out of the blue. "I'm here to make sure some things happen, and some things don't. The company, the institute, we work for is part of the plan, but not all of it," Eddie says while looking at Françoise. Françoise slightly nods.

"Wait a minute," I say, "Françoise, you talked about another traveller before dinner, is this what you were talking about?"

"Somewhat so," she says, "I think I know part of it, and for the rest I was just starting to find out."

"You know the difference between the three of you?" Eddie asks.

"We know the superhumans amongst us, if that is what you mean," I say.

"It's in your brains," Eddie says and turns towards me. "You have developed a natural way beyond regular humans, while your wife has a genetically modified brain, and your daughter has the best of both worlds, naturally. Apart from that you're normal humans. Well, special humans, but normal humans, you know?"

"How special do you mean?" Marie-Isobelle asks.

"How normal do you mean?" I ask.

Eighteen

Françoise had a worried look on her face. The check-up at the hospital didn't go as expected. Elle was preparing lunch when Françoise came in. "Hey sunshine," she said.

"With clouds," Françoise replied while she hung away her coat.

A week later it turned out that it got even worse, very unusual, and Françoise had lost her baby. As strong as she seemed to be, yet she stayed home for about the next two weeks, not interested in visitors, alone with her sorrow, alone with her pain, alone with her tears. Alone with Elle. The pain for the loss, and the joy for Elle. The contrast was tearing her apart, but they kept talking, and finally also told me.

It touched me deeper than I expected. I was glad Françoise had Elle with her. I was glad I had my wife to talk to, to learn to let go, to learn to accept life's beauty and ugliness. There is beauty in real pain, yes I know how weird that would sound. I thought it related to how deep it touched me, it touched me at the core, even though I felt a barrier between me and Françoise. A wall, something like *"Le Passe Muraille"*, where you know exactly which direction to go, but you can't get through. You're stuck.

On the day of the burial my wife and I had decided to go together. A tiny little white coffin, again I was touched by beauty and ugliness. I thought of the painting by Frank Bramley, "For of Such is the Kingdom of Heaven". Then I walked up to Françoise and held her; after a few seconds, like a flashback I felt our walk along the canals of Amsterdam. The light of the lanterns, her arm in my arm, her smile, her eyes, her kiss, her warmth. Françoise slightly seemed to lose of her balance, so I held her even closer. And then I opened my eyes, I saw Elle pregnant, I saw my wife pregnant. It felt as if the world was moving away from me. And then as if it moved back and everything became one. I had to be strong for everyone, so I did. Françoise had to be strong for herself, so she did, so she unbelievably did. I realised I truly loved her. I realised I understood nothing and everything, all at the same time. It felt more real than reality itself...

Nineteen

Eddie looks at us and smiles.

"So, now you know there's one more thing I need to explain," he says and sits back in the couch, "sometimes I feel myself as the gatekeeper, jumping between different realities, different realities that act in different times, at different times, at different time speeds. It's not magic, it's science from the future, but still far from as easy as it sounds." Eddie takes his bag and slightly opens it.

"This is the time machine," he says, "we call it the Transformer."

"What does it do?" Marie-Isobelle asks.

"It works like a controlled, inside-out black hole-mantle, a transport bubble, so to speak."

Silence.

"And the agent, the security guy I just mentioned, also seems to have one, though that one might be slightly different, as he is also slightly different."

"Ehm, if I understand correctly, I heard you would be slightly different, actually more than just slightly, that's what the agent told my friend Chisato," Marie-Isobelle says while she moves forward.

I feel a bit uncomfortable as the situation seems a bit awkward.

"OK," says Eddie, "I understand this has become quite a lot to take in, so what I suggest for you, for us, is to think about all I've told you, and I will think about what you've told me, so we can find a way forward."

"OK, but let's not take too long, for I think there will be more questions still than answers," I say.

Suddenly I realise that the room had gotten slightly dark, as the auto-lights are gently switching on, and I see both Marie-Isobelle's and Françoise's face light up.

"Let's talk about it again tomorrow, during daytime," Françoise suggests.

Eddie agrees, takes his bag, thanks for the tea and excuses himself for the sudden visit, and leaves.

We're back in the living room, still impressed by all we heard in the last few hours.

"What have we gotten ourselves into?" Françoise says.

"I think it came to us, it's not like we chose it," I say.

"What do they want from us?" Marie-Isobelle responds.

"I don't know," Françoise says, and walks towards the kitchen to make more tea. She chooses the red tea tin, her favourite colour and her favourite tea, sencha almond & cinnamon. The small distraction helps her to make up her mind, it seems.

"Who do you trust?" Marie-Isobelle then asks. "The agent that visited Chisato, or Eddie?"

"I don't know," Françoise says again, "at this moment I don't know who to trust anymore."

I walk up to Françoise and give her a hug, Marie-Isobelle joins in, a greenish, reddish, purplish bubble forms around us. It feels totally warm, comfortable, safe, almost as if it could just lift off...

The next day Françoise leaves early in the morning to go to the institute. At the entrance she notices a few more people than usual behind the desk. A friendly "Good morning," and she walks over to her office. One of the people behind the front desk starts following her. "Excuse me," and then again, "Excuse me," and then Françoise stops and turns around.

"Yes," Françoise says.

"We think there is something wrong with your office."

"What do you mean?" As it is only a few steps further to her office, Françoise walks on and opens the door. Only to find that it won't open.

"I tried to tell you," the desk lady says. "We've noticed a few offices are acting up, including the library. Security technicians are already looking into it."

Françoise stays a little longer, but then decides to go back home. Then she notices Eddie, sitting on the other end of the hallway. Somewhat obscured, but he's wearing the same clothes as yesterday, which is what made him easier to spot. He didn't notice Françoise, but she walks up to him. Right next to him, she takes a seat.

"You smell," she says.

Eddie turns towards her. "You too, lovely."

"Good morning Eddie."

"Good morning Françoise."

"So what's going on? Where have you been? You really smell as if you've been sleeping in a can of worms."

"Haha, you're almost right, I slept in my car. When I came home yesterday I noticed the weirdo agent hanging around, so I decided to avoid him, and slept in my car. Sorry for the smell, but you'll get used to it fairly quickly." Eddie laughs, and Françoise laughs with him, though with a frown. She moves slightly away from Eddie, but he doesn't notice.

"Is your office also locked?" she then asks.

"Yes," he answers. After a little pause he continues, and moves slightly towards Françoise. "When you time-travel into the unknown future you disappear, or seem to disappear into it, I don't exactly know, somewhat like a black hole. However, a higher 'God-like awareness' can tap into future information, timeless information, without actually travelling into it. The issue is that the few humans with the brain talent like your daughter might learn how to do that. I think that's what he's after."

"Who?"

"That agent guy, our security..." Eddie stops talking, the lady from the front desk walks up to them.

"Excuse me, your offices are available again," she says.

"Thank you," Françoise responds, and then turns to Eddie again. "I heard that you can only travel back, but not into the future?"

"Well yes," Eddie answers, "for obvious reasons I think nobody can travel back from a very distant future to give us this kind of unknown, structural, changing information, otherwise that same future would be destroyed, unless that information is kept in a very small, strictly protected, secret community, which actually does exist. But they are a danger to themselves, well, as you know the risk of corruption, you know, selfish private gain or absolute social power. You know..., politicians and the like."

Françoise looks totally absorbed, but after a few seconds looks up again.

"Wait a minute," she then says. "What about professor Kodaira? Did you... really kill him?"

Eddie looks at her as calmly as possible.

"No, I didn't," he says. "I know they were looking for me, but I already talked to them, and explained as far as I could."

"Then why were they looking for you? You were in that security footage, right?"

"I was actually trying to protect him, but I was too late."

"So, you could go further back in time to prevent it?"

"Well, that's the catch, I cannot go back in time to prevent actual deaths. But strictly speaking, as contradictory as it may sound, I can prevent people from being born."

Twenty

Elle and Françoise had decided to go away for a little while, not too far, just away. Simple and relaxed. They chose to go to a little old town close to the border with Germany. A little town called Doesburg.

"Let's sit under that tree," Elle said, and so they sat on a bench under an old oak tree, watching down the street. They watched the old buildings, the old people, bicycles, the canopy of leaves and the sun shining through.

"Let's have an ice cream," Françoise said. "You can stay here, I'll get them." And off she went, it was only twenty metres away though. Elle just sat there quietly, enjoying the calmness of this little place. She looked at the colours of the bricks, a deep orange, warm and even warmer with the sun heating them up. The rattling noise of car tyres on the cobblestones was ruining the serene quietness, as a car came towards her. Françoise stepped outside the ice cream shop while the car was speeding up, moving towards her, she jumped to the side, holding on to the ice creams that were still in her hands.

"Hey!" Elle shouted, while seeing the car moving on.

"Idiot!" Françoise shouted. Quickly though the quietness was restored, even though some old people seemed to have noticed, just shaking their heads, as if it happened every day.

"I'm glad you didn't buy the ice creams," Françoise said.

"I'm glad you're OK, are you?"

"Yes, yes, forget about the maniac," she said with a hint of a smile. More a smile of mutual encouragement towards Elle though, than as an expression of her true happiness. With one hand holding an ice cream, with the other hand holding Françoise, Elle actually was happy.

They strolled around the village till lunchtime and found a little restaurant with a small terrace outside in the gentle morning sun, "De Liefde".

"Love," Françoise said.

I woke up with a horrible feeling and it followed me all through the morning. At lunchtime I decided to take the day off, and there I was, sitting in an armchair with a cup of tea, making no sense of it all. It was as if I'd finally allowed a sense of guilt to come to the surface, I saw it, and I didn't feel comfortable with what I saw. I saw me, causing pain. I saw me caring, loving, enjoying, and still causing pain. The headache was getting worse. I closed my eyes, folded my hands and leaned with my head against them. Guilt. Was it guilt? At some point I felt proud. Was I an asshole? Thoughts were twirling in my head, colours were twirling in my head. Orange-red and swirls of green. Deep colours, deep, not cold, but warm. It surprised me, but then they turned cold, red with a hint of blue, cold and somewhat scary.

When I opened my eyes it looked as if the colours were still there. I thought a few sips of tea would help me get out of it. It did, somehow. I saw the situation more clearly, but it didn't make me feel any better. Three women pregnant, three lovely women pregnant, and one of them lost her baby. What was next?

Elle was just finishing her mustard soup when Françoise alarmedly looked to the side. There was that rattling noise again, car tyres coming closer at great speed. Now they could also hear the engine noise, speeding up towards them. Françoise jumped up from her chair, grabbed Elle and pulled her away from the roadside. The car clipped her chair with a loud bang and cracking noises and the chair landed in front of the neighbouring house, actually more what was left of the chair. The car sped off, while Françoise had had a glimpse of the driver, they had looked each other straight in the eyes.

While the owner of the restaurant came running outside to check on what happened and on the ladies, to see they were not physically harmed, he offered them a drink inside but they declined. He asked them to wait for the police to arrive, and then they decided to have a drink after all. A sparkling water for Elle, and a French coffee for Françoise. This wasn't just an accident, or just an idiot, they concluded.

"I have seen him before," Françoise said, "but I don't know where."

Elle looked at her and frowned.

"I remember him," she said. "He was in the hospital when you had your check-up."

"Yes," Françoise said slowly, as if she was thinking of something else, or rather in something else, their shared consciousness... They both went quiet, while looking at each other, and without a sound they both left the restaurant. In the distance they could hear the police car coming, rattling over the cobblestones.

I felt relieved, my headache was gone, but still I somehow was feeling alert, more than just aware. I thought of Françoise, of what she would be doing now. I thought of how we met, her birthday party, how I woke up in her bed. I realised how beautiful she was, and how conflicted I was. I thought of Joan and how much I would have hurt her and how she acted as if she was not hurt. She was pregnant and was enjoying it all the way. Pregnant women indeed become like warriors, I thought, warriors on a mission.

Elle still looked stunning, if you wouldn't know she was pregnant, you just might miss it. Just a small, gentle bulge, adding to the gentle curves she had already. It actually made her even more beautiful. They had moved back to their hotel, in a close-by town called Doetinchem. With a deep sigh they both took a seat in the lobby and ordered a tea for two, with some nibbles. It was quiet, but they liked it that way. On the table was a small booklet, Elle picked it up and started to read.

"You need to hear this," she said, and started to read out loud.

*"Longing's lurchings have gashed a mighty rift
in soul's torn surface, normally so smooth;
emerging from oblivion's grey ooze,
wreck upon wreck, old memories now drift;*

*and madness, on whose wave-crests' flexed awryness
in flickering dance wild fantasies abound,
its sledge seems to knock crumbling slabs of ground
loose from a continent of quaking I-ness.*

*Rising to ecstasy from deep despair
around the fearful one held captive there
insistent rings of waves constrict at will...*

*free Self-Awareness though of Brahman's Being,
that witnesses its worldly fears unfleeing,
drifts in triumphant balance, calmly still."*

"I'm sorry, I missed the first few lines," Françoise said. Can I read it again?"

Elle gave her the booklet.

"It was written in the early 19th century, it says," Elle said when she noticed Françoise had finished reading it.

"Johan Andreas dèr Mouw," Françoise reads. "Never heard of him before."

"He was a professor at the Lyceum, when this building

was a Lyceum, a school for smart, talented children. Pre-university education," the waitress explained while serving the tea.

"Ah, thank you," Françoise said kindly.

"Oh, you can keep the booklet," the waitress said. "It's for our guests."

"Ah, great, thank you," Elle responded.

Françoise leaned back, and started reading more. It seemed she had already forgotten what happened just a few hours before.

"*Good*," Elle thought.

Twenty-one

I park the car in front of the M-institute, the lady at the front desk recognises me and after a polite greeting ceremony I explain that I've parked my car only for a few minutes to pick up my wife for lunch. I walk through the hall towards Françoise's office and see that the door is open. I go in and see Françoise sitting behind her desk.

"Good afternoon darling, ready for lunch?" Then I see the look on her face, as she points behind me. The shelves are empty...

"They took everything," she says, "it makes no sense, we have, I have everything in digital copies."

Then I see that on the other side of the room, in front of the window, Eddie is standing, looking outside.

"It's the same in my office," he says. "Clean as a whistle, cleaner than ever before."

Another man enters the room, he's dressed in uniform.

"Hi Karl," Françoise says. "You remember Karl? He is our head of security," she continues to explain to me.

"Nice to meet you again Sir."

"Nice to meet you too Karl."

"Hi Eddie."

Eddie nods.

"Right," Karl says. "There is nothing on our security footage, not even a triggered sensor in the hallway."

Eddie looks at Françoise, and Françoise looks at me. I think we all have the same thought.

"If you'll excuse me, I'm having a meeting with my boss, our boss, in a minute. I'll let you know after that. Nice again to meet you Sir," and off Karl goes again. It seems it's one of those rare moments where the memory loss from an old accident comes to haunt me. I really could not remember him, luckily it happens with only very few people. Mostly though with people from the M-institute it seems.

Eddie closes the door and leans against it. He looks out and then down towards his shoes.

"I don't know," he says. "Did he take all of that as some kind of trophy? He could just have copied all digital files?"

Françoise starts laughing.

"It's so ridiculous, it makes absolutely no sense!" And after a little pause, "But for God's sake, he's not just been in my office, he's been in and out of my private life as if it means nothing!"

Then it's silent. Eddie just looks, and says nothing.

"Shall I take you to lunch?" I ask Françoise.

"Yes, let's get out of here," she replies.

She is wearing a thin fabric, white t-shirt, maybe a pyjama, with nothing under it, and is standing in front of the bookcase, to the left I see a lofty room, the others sitting on the couch, amused, talking with each other. And just when I put back a book right in front of her, she put back a book right in front of me, on a higher shelf. Before I could move my arm back, she had caught it under her arm. My right hand is on top of her right breast, and she's holding my arm right there. Nobody seems to notice, and I'm in total confusion.

It was just a dream, and yet I'm still confused. Who was she?

Françoise has taken the day off, and so do I. We'll try to get our lives in line again. So we decide that today we'll take a scenic ride to Strasbourg, find a nice place to have a drink, and visit some art galleries, just for the two of us.

After some forty or fifty minutes we already see a nice spot to have our chocolate drink, with a view towards the Rhine valley. It actually feels very energising, sitting under a tree, watching the busy city in the distance. The contrast is very amusing. Meanwhile we lean against each other and against the tree.

"It feels like a gentle treesome," I say, Françoise laughs and gives me a kiss. After some twenty minutes we decide to move on towards Strasbourg. After some thirty more minutes, while slowing down for other traffic, I see a poster along the road advertising for the *Musée des Beaux-Arts* in Strasbourg. To celebrate the re-opening after the renovation that had taken more than a year, they had a special painting on loan for the next six months: Leonardo da Vinci's "Salvator Mundi". So, we decide to slightly change our plans, as it already had been a while since we had been to the museum.

On *Quai Schoepflin* Françoise waves to the other side of the canal where we had lived for a few months. Along *Rue du Parchemin*, and to the left *Rue des Pucelles*, the old German "*Jumpfergass*", where Françoise and I first kissed.

I had always wondered how it would have been to have lived here, when it still was Germany, and from one moment to the other, your house would be in France... And today it almost seems like Strasbourg is getting its own little Chinatown, right next to the "*Jumpfergass*"...

Soon I would have to find a parking spot, as, even for the

fact that public transport is great in Strasbourg, there still are lots of private cars around. Just at the end of *Rue des Juifs* I find a good spot. Next to the *cathedrale* we're having a cappuccino, and then we we're ready for the "Salvator Mundi". Because I'm a member of the "*Société des Amis des Arts et des Musées de Strasbourg*" we don't have to pay the full price and decide to walk straight to it. My fear is confirmed though, just as with Da Vinci's "Mona Lisa" when I saw it in Paris, here it also is crowded and the star of the show is very hard to see. I'm determined though, so slowly, and with a little bit of straightforwardness we arrive in front of it.

"Is it what you expected?" Françoise asks.

I hesitate, I don't want to say that I'm a bit disappointed. I'm glad though that I finally have seen it, the crystal orb, representing life and existence beyond our realities, repre-senting the living orb, of higher life, of higher existence, of highest existence? Da Vinci knew, and only very few of his contemporaries, as we all learned.

"I'm glad I've seen it," I say, and stay for a little longer to see what I could feel from it.

After we left I realised I was so focused on seeing Da Vinci, that I forgot to notice the renovations, but then again, it doesn't really matter now, I'm thinking more about the orb. Shortly after the opening, I heard a security guard say, there already had been an attack on the painting, someone with a small laser pistol, but they noticed before he could do any real damage to the painting. Some even said it had been a publicity stunt, who knows?

As it still is the busy summer tourist season we decide to visit again in a few months. We walk back along the *cathedrale* towards *Rue des Hallebardes*, which is where we notice disrupting shifts in our awareness, both Françoise and I, at the same time. It's as if we went back and forth between moments in time, one moment we saw this, and the other moment we saw that. We walk further and everything seemed normal, we walk back to the same spot and we see the same disruptions again. But as we can not see what could have caused it we walk on, a bit annoyed by it, but then further on also by the number of multinational shops that you still see in every metropole around the westernised world.

"For a significant number of humans it seems awareness is growing, but for the majority it certainly isn't," I say, slightly annoyed.

The AI community certainly isn't helping, but then

again, their presence seems to be diminishing, which I think is a good thing. I prefer MODUs, quite a lot actually, I think smiling! I love my MODUs!

"Is he following us?" Françoise asks.

I turn around and see a man in a dark coat and with a small shoulder bag. He also stops and seems to look around to see where he is. The coat actually looks out of season, clearly not a summer coat, especially not on this day.

"I bet that bag is some kind of Transformer," Françoise says.

"I bet that disruption we just saw, had to do with him," I reply.

We walk over to *Place Gutenberg*, and take a ride on the almost ancient merry-go-round and see what he does.

"He doesn't know what to do," Françoise says laughing.

We watch him walking past and disappear around the corner. We're actually having fun on the merry-go-round and feel silly when we get off. For a moment we don't care about the guy following us. Just for a moment...

"Oh, there he is," I say, watching him watching us.

"Hey guys!" I hear from behind us.

It's Eddie.

"Yup, it's him," he says. "Let me handle this," he continues.

Eddie walks up to him, and we see the dark guy change his posture, standing firm and alert, but acting relaxed.

"Hi mate!" Eddie says to him.

"Hi mate," he replies.

"I think we know what you're doing here," Eddie says.

"Are you sure?" he replies. "Are you sure what you're getting yourself into here?"

Eddie just looks at him.

"I know who you are, what you do, and even why. But there's a problem. You're wrong," the dark guy says while he takes a step forward from under the obscuring gallery.

From a distance we watch the dark agent put his hand on his bag, and we see Eddie do the same while taking a step back. It's like a stand-off that you'd see in an old Western movie. The agent touches a screen and taps on it. Instantaneously a hull of light covers his body, and grows larger into some kind of bubble, still following the contours of his body though. Eddie also switches on his Transformer, slowly forming a round bubble around him. Now he steps towards the agent, touching his bubble. The agent zaps away, with Eddie attached to him.

Dematerialised they both zoom out of their 4D reality. Eddie clings to him and does not let go. With his mind's eye Eddie can see time stretching around them and forming patterns, sometimes even familiar forms as they sometimes slow down and then suddenly increase their speed or go around sharp corners. It becomes unfamiliar terrain for Eddie, and he feels it becomes harder to hold on and keep up.

When the dark agent starts to speed up to go beyond Eddie's time zone, Eddie sticks himself even stronger to the agent. The agent tries to pull Eddie into the unknown future, but when they reach Eddie's time zone the agent seems to get stuck, Eddie's attachment actually stops him from going further. They both are stuck in Eddie's time.

"OK, calm down," the agent communicates. "Let's settle down here and synchronise."

Very much on alert for any tricks Eddie synchronises with the agent. They land on a beach, unknown to both, but in Eddie's own time.

Twenty-two

"Watch out for Eddie, he's fooling you. He's dangerous," the message said. I didn't recognise the voice and after asking Joan to listen to the message and the voice, she didn't recognise it either. Françoise didn't respond to my call, so I left a message for her.

A few days later she answered it.

"Sorry for not responding sooner," she said. "Elle and I needed a few days off, away from it all."

"And, how did it work out for you both?"

"Good, good," she said. "Well, not as simple as that, but good anyway." I heard somewhat of a smile in her voice.

"We've been attacked, but further from that, we had a great time, lots of talking time. I'm happy for Elle, and she knows it. I'm also worried for Elle, because of the attack."

"What attack? What happened?" I asked her.

"A car tried to hit us, probably even twice," she said.

"A car?"

"I clearly saw the driver, and Elle said he was also in the hospital when I had a check-up, on the baby. I know it sounds ridiculous, but we actually think he may be responsible for the death of our baby." The smile was gone from her voice, I heard a small, nervous tremble.

"Are you OK now Françoise?"

"Yes, yes, it's just a moment, Elle and I talked about it endlessly," she said with a little smile again. "I think we're doing fine."

Clearly her kindness was showing, she doesn't want me to worry, I thought.

"You're a hero," I told her, "a lovely hero."

She started to laugh.

"You're a darling," she replied, "a lovely darling."

We both laughed out loud.

"I miss you," she said.

I hesitated for a moment, but then replied, "Yes, I miss you too."

Silence, a few seconds that sounded like forever.

"I'm so sorry," she said, "I did not want to trick you. But, I was so glad it happened, even though I think we may have been manipulated, or even trapped, into our meeting. I do love you, with all of my heart."

I didn't know what to say, so I just said what I knew to be true: "I love you too," with a huge sense of compromise.

Again it was silent for a second or two.

"I wish you were here, right now," she said softly and slowly.

"I'm sorry, I can't do that," I said.

"I know, it would just be so wonderful, to feel you, to kiss you, to have you with me, yes, to touch you, for you to touch me."

My head started spinning, I imagined the words she was saying, like a spell, and yet, I knew it was not possible, not there, not then, or maybe ever again?

"I feel you," I said, "I feel your warmth, your body, your lips, just to hear your voice already makes me feel... I don't know, I don't have a word for it, happy, warm, hot, complete? I don't know. You're wonderful."

I thought she sensed my concern.

"Are you coming to Amsterdam again?" she asked.

"Of course," I said, knowing that it's not that simple.

"I understand about your wife, about Joan," she said. "I understand that you do love her, of course. It doesn't make a difference for me."

A huge sense of relief came over me, as if, in that very second, everything fell in place.

"You are beautiful," I said.

"Thank you," she said.

I thought about holding her in my arms, right at that very moment.

"You know, Eddie sends his greetings to you, I saw him half an hour ago," Françoise then said, "he acts as if he's somewhere else in his mind, not here with us."

"Why are you saying that?" I asked.

"I don't know, it just felt weird. Weird, but also significant, for some reason. I don't know."

I could listen to her voice all day, without hearing a word, just her voice, just her melody, she was such a joy to listen to. Or just being in the connection, being on one end, knowing she's on the other end.

"Are you still there?" she then asked.

"Yes, yes, I'm here," I said.

There she was, finally! Finally I had found her, in Paris, even though this one was white, but in a very good condition, almost like new, just as the 4C I had. White with yellow brake callipers, I liked it quite a lot already.

"Do you like it?" the salesman asked.

"Yes I do," I replied. I tried to ignore him as to avoid the typical sales pitch, but then he offered me to take a seat in the car. I climbed in, one foot first and then slid into position. He then gave me the key, to have a drive around the block. I knew I already was sold, but he didn't know that. Or maybe he did, as I might be in the exact target group for this car. But then again, from what I knew that group was quite broad, mostly romantics though, romantics with a good mind and good taste, haha. He introduced himself as Casper, but it was a name of convenience, as he explained his Chinese name was too complicated, which was something I had noticed that a few friends who lived in Paris's Chinatown also did, actually like their ancestors did since they came to live in Paris, a tradition from just a few hundred years ago?

As this was a factory super hydrogen conversion it came with a factory certification and the Alfa Romeo Hydrogen Programme Warranty, he said. Yeah, but I was sold already.

"My grandfather had one," he continued. "My father told me how he always loved it when his father took him for a ride around the countryside."

I smiled, "My grandfather had a Porsche 911, my father said the same thing about him, and the car." I showed him a picture of my father as a kid behind the steering wheel of his father's Porsche. I always treasured it in a very special way.

"Chase good memories, and make good memories," he said when he stood up from beside the car and opened the showroom door. I turned the key and about an hour later I was the new owner of the white Alfa 4C.

"Happy memories," I said when I closed the door and drove off with the happy sounds of hydrogen. I behaved myself well, for a while...

Twenty-three

"Let me take off my zapp-pack," the agent says.

It looks as if the tension becomes less. They both seem to feel confident, but on alert. They walk a little back and forth, keeping an eye both on each other and the scenery around them.

"It's quiet here," the agent says.

Eddie doesn't respond immediately, he seems a little bit confused. "Yeah, yeah," he says.

"You know," the agent continues, "the thing is, if you guys keep doing this, we won't have the second coming of the Lord, ever. Do you understand what that means?"

Now Eddie looks him straight in the eyes, focused, as if he looks straight through him. He's studying the agent.

"Oh God," he says, "you're one of those Armageddon fanatics. No matter how, no matter the consequences, you want this to happen because you believe you're right. You believe your selfish, immature longing is right. Right?"

The agent finally starts to notice that Eddie is not there as a human, as he's a physical projection of self.

"I'm not here, this isn't happening the way you think it

is," Eddie continues.

"I already thought so," the agent replies.

"Who are you, and where do you come from?" Eddie then asks.

"I'm Ben, and I'm a senior time agent of the Star of David group. That's a neat trick you do, and pretty safe I suppose?"

"I don't know the Star of David group, I suppose it's something from the future?"

Ben smiles. "Yes, but then again, in the future not everything is better." He seems to be trying to create a gentle mood of confidence. "Because of cost reduction and specialisation we're not as widely talented as your generations. Fascinating to finally see you from this close."

Eddie looks at him with a little frown between his eyes. He realises that, if this is true he himself may be more powerful than he thought.

"Not every progress is an improvement," Eddie says.

"Operation Kodaira was a significant step into developing higher humans, superhumans," agent Ben explains. "Because of that we risk creating a human society that is so harmonious that the Second Coming will not happen. Well, that's what we believe."

Eddie listens with a sense of coldness surrounding him.

"It's not my purpose to hurt you," Ben continues.

"I'm not sure I understand how that works, but from what I see I think you're lying," Eddie replies.

In the distance, close to the water, a hovering orb is watching, but both Eddie and agent Ben do not notice it.

In a distance, far away in space and time, Eddie realises this is getting more serious than expected. He opens his eyes and allows his projected clone to function in auto-mode. There's a small shiver and the clone takes over. Agent Ben did notice and decides to zap away, this time Eddie does not respond in time to follow, which he could not have done anyway if the agent went through the future time barrier. It's unclear where he went.

Eddie gets up, and walks out of the door of his lab. Nobody else is in the hallway and Eddie walks to Françoise's office to see if she's there. She's not, and it's still empty, empty and unlocked. He decides to walk in anyway and sits on the wide window frame. "*A trophy hunter*," he thinks to himself and sighs. But he didn't take any of the very personal belongings of Françoise, the pictures, diplomas, certificates, or actually copies thereof, they're still there.

Then Karl comes in. "Hi Eddie," he says.

"Hi Karl."

And a second or two later, Françoise follows.

"Hey, it's Eddie!"

"Hey Françoise!"

"It looks OK Karl, thanks."

"You don't need anything else?"

"No, thank you."

And out goes Karl again.

Françoise takes a seat beside Eddie, they turn their faces towards each other.

"It's bad," Eddie says.

"How bad? Françoise asks.

"Sinbad," Eddie replies with a laugh, but then quickly returns to a serious tone.

"It's bad enough to kill for," he continues.

"Why?" Françoise asks.

"Because he's willing to kill for it."

"For what?"

"He's like an Armageddon fanatic from the future. Well, he works for Armageddon fanatics, and they see us as a threat. He, or they, believe we could be making humanity into such good beings, that the Second Coming won't happen."

"What?"

"Yes, what, that's what I also thought. He's from my future, but with simplified talents, an economy version of me," he says with a slightly smiling face.

"Oh, come on," Françoise says. "Do they come simpler than you?"

It's quiet for a second, then they both burst out in laughter.

"Yes, I understand it's serious," she then says with a slightly nervous tone.

"They have killed before, you know," Eddie says with concern in his voice.

"I get it, I get it," Françoise says.

Marie-Isobelle is sitting outside, under an umbrella, half relaxing, half studying. She has a mellow aura around her. Sometimes I see her smiling, with a hint of laughing. Maybe she's not studying as I thought she would be.

"Hey sunshine, here's a cool drink for you," and I give her a glass of apple juice.

"Thanks dad," she replies with a smile.

While I sit next to her it looks as if her aura expands towards me, and then even includes me.

"I love you," she says.

"I love you too," I say. "Always."

She reaches out her hand and we have a handhug. I'm proud of us.

"I was just talking with Chisato," she says, "she asked me to say hi to you for her. I think she's doing fine."

"Great, what is she doing now?" I ask her.

"Oh, I don't know, she's in her shop."

"How is she doing?"

"She's doing fine, we actually did talk about that visit she had, from the guy who told her to be careful with Eddie."

"Right," I say, "I would not be surprised if that was the same guy your mother and I saw in Strasbourg."

"Hm, me too," Marie-Isobelle responds.

"You know your mother is bringing him for dinner tonight?"

"No," she responds, surprised.

"Yup, and we'll make dinner."

Marie-Isobelle throws me a look as if she's too busy with other things.

"Yup," I say again, with a smile.

She throws colours at me, like snowballs.

"Hey! Mai! I actually can feel those!"

Marie-Isobelle starts laughing, as it seems she was surprised by that too. It almost feels as if they not just splash on my body, but also penetrate. Marie-Isobelle laughs even harder.

"I love you dad!" she says, while I instinctively duck away, but after a few seconds let it all come to me. And then the most amazing thing happens: I can throw them back, something got triggered in me, I can throw them back!

"Dad!" Marie-Isobelle shouts with excitement.

The wind blows gently through the trees. Small birds are chirping away, and in the distance is a Cuckoo. Only thing missing is Françoise, but she'll be home soon.

Twenty-four

I looked at "Pygmalion and Galatea", the painting by Jean Léon Gérôme; and my car, and back. Somehow I thought the white colour made the 4C even better, more alive, more statuesque, more alive and statuesque.

"Should I be jealous?" Joan asked.

"Hm, maybe," I said with a smile.

"Well yes, she is beautiful, isn't she?" she said while she walked up to her and gently let her hand follow the curved contours.

"Hm, should I be jealous now?" I asked.

"Hm, maybe," she said laughing.

I made a step towards her and she put her arms around me. In between us was another beautifully curved contour, keeping us at a small distance. But we hugged and kissed nevertheless and it even felt as if the little new human wanted to be part of it. I kissed her belly, and it responded. Beautiful.

"Oh, happy Celtic New Year," I said.

"Aha, is it that time of year again?" she replied and laughed.

I gave Joan a kiss, and another kiss on her belly. Again it felt as if the belly responded.

"I think the baby felt that," I said.

"Sure she did," Joan said.

"She?"

"Yes, I think it's a she," she said, laughing. "As beautiful as only she can be."

"Let's go inside, it's getting a bit chilly."

Hand in hand we walked to the house. I looked at her belly, it looked like a few more months before the baby would arrive. I felt excited, and scared, but also full of trust, we would make it happen. I felt as if I could see things even more clearly than usual. It was as if my awareness was added with an extra layer, warm and caring. Or was it my wife? Joan just smiled...

High above us a Sentinel was observing.

We went inside and I walked to the kitchen to make us some tea.

"How is Françoise doing?" my wife suddenly asked, after she had comfortably placed herself on the sofa.

"I actually don't know, but the last time we spoke she seemed to do be doing alright."

That is when I noticed a letter laying on the bar. I picked

it up, it was from Françoise.

"There's a letter here from Françoise," I said.

"Oh, I'm sorry," Joan said, "didn't I tell you it came this morning?"

I opened it, but then decided to read it later. I felt my heart beat faster.

After we had almost finished our tea I decided to start reading the letter after all. I opened it again and could smell a hint of perfume. I recognised it, yes, it was Françoise's. On white paper, it was a handwritten letter and I started reading the words I would never forget.

After a few minutes I looked up from the paper sheets, and I noticed my wife looking at me. I felt very confused and of course Joan noticed.

"How is she?" she kindly asked, again.

"She's good. She is good," I replied. After a few seconds I continued. "Emotional ups and downs, but energetic, she thinks about us, you, me, us, but then again, in general she says she's increasingly feeling better, balanced, yeah, she's good, she says."

I didn't tell my wife about the last part of the letter.

"...Right now I'd love to whisper so many loving words in your ear, quietly and softly and tender. OK, just imagine I'd be doing that. I'm holding you and my forces flow into you and maybe can help you. How are you? Is it still going up and down? How are you feeling?

Let me kiss you, hold you, love you. I'd love to hear from you.

*Your Françoise **

(That doesn't mean just one kiss! Right? It's a little representative for so many, many, many)

*Sleep well! **

On the back of the envelope, that was made from an old paper magazine page, I noticed a few artistic, printed words, upside down, of which I wasn't sure if it had any relevance or meaning:

"monter le temps précieusement
à pied, à cheval, en bateau..."

She was right, my emotional balance was still going up and down. I didn't get the meaning of it all. She already had said that if I hadn't been married it would have made it very different the first time we had met. She loves me, I love her, and she respects the love I have for my wife, and my wife for me. She has lost her baby, our baby, and my wife is happily pregnant with ours. How messed up and in a way beautiful at the same time, I thought.

The room was humming with gentleness. I watched Joan, watching me.

"Come here," she said softly.

We kissed and hugged. I didn't show my tears, for her, and neither did she.

The next morning I woke up with a sense of pride: two of the most beautiful women loved me dearly. Followed by a sense of shame and guilt, of how I would be hurting those two most beautiful women at the same time. I looked at Joan, still sleeping, and I thought I saw the baby moving. I gently kissed the baby, and Joan opened her eyes with a smile.

"Good morning," I said.

"Good morning," she replied, with a kiss.

This is how it went on for the next few days, weeks.

Almost like clockwork the light orb came hovering by, but I didn't notice, and neither did Joan. Neither did Elle notice the light orb checking up on her. Neither did any of us know it actually was Eddie...

Eddie had changed. Somehow his capabilities had changed, not only could he move through time, dimensions, now he could also change form. It wasn't clear if his changing form was a cause or an effect. He wasn't using his Transformer anymore. Instead of using the Transformer to create a bubble, Eddie now could transpose directly into a light orb, somekind of double existence. Something definitely had changed, but we didn't know. And we didn't know when Eddie came to visit us the next morning.

"Good morning! Did I wake you up?" Eddie asked on the phone.

"No, no," I said. "How are you?"

"I'm good, thank you. You know, I'll be in the neighbourhood today, would it suit you if I came to visit you?"

"Sure, no problem, we'll be here all day. What time did you plan to come over?"

"Before or after lunch?" Eddie said.

"You can have lunch with us," I said.

"Sounds great, around 12:30 then?"

"Good, see you then. Oh, you know where we live, do you?"

"Yes, yes, Françoise explained it to me."

Hearing her name made me pause for a little moment.

"OK, see you later!"

"See you later!"

Joan and I finished our breakfast and looked outside at the slightly foggy world, and a clear blue sky above it. It looked like it would be a wonderful day.

Eddie arrived in splendid grandeur, somehow he had changed, grown up maybe?

"Want some tea or coffee?" I asked when he entered our house.

"Yes please," Eddie said. "A tea please."

Eddie entered the room where Joan was already sitting.

"How are you? Nice to see you again," Eddie said.

"Nice to see you again," Joan replied. "Please take a seat."

Eddie sat down at the table where Joan and I already had prepared the lunch.

"You look very much alive, radiant, " Eddie said to Joan. "I see you and the baby are doing fine?"

"Oh yes," Joan replied, "between every little hiccup."

She laughed, which made her belly go up and down a little too abruptly, but she immediately calmed down.

"I see, I see," Eddie said, smiling.

"So, what brings you to our neck of the woods?' I asked while I poured him some tea.

"Oh, I had a business meeting this morning in Strasbourg, tomorrow morning in Stuttgart and after that up north to Berlin. As you've seen I'm following your example by travelling slowly by car and enjoying the journey from a different perspective."

"I'm surprised," I said. "You've actually changed, did you?"

"Some people do learn," Eddie replied, smiling.

We continued our lunch in a relaxed atmosphere, more relaxed and kind than I had expected. The change was keeping me thinking, everything seemed to be changing so fast. Was time changing? Was time really speeding up? After we had finished our lunch we had a look at Eddie's classical S4, enjoyed its colours and style. I took a seat behind the wheel, on the passenger seat was a backpack that I had seen before. And then he left for Stuttgart, where the next morning his business meeting didn't seem like a business meeting at all. The meeting was with another nice couple, well educated, well dressed, living a comfortable life, and the woman was pregnant. They all seemed to have met before.

Meanwhile in Amsterdam Elle and Agnes were sitting on a terrace watching the people moving by. Elle's pregnancy was slightly further than Joan's, but was less visible. Elle and Agnes both were very much aware though, that there was a Sentinel watching over them. What they both did not know, is that this Sentinel actually was Eddie.

The agent was back in town, acting like a regular tourist, standing out and blending in. He seemed to be aware of Eddie's presence, as he moved along without actually doing something.

"How long from now?" Agnes asked.

"About six weeks," Elle responded.

"You look so great, so beautiful," Agnes said.

"Thank you," Elle replied with a blush and a smile.

"You look like you're glowing," Agnes said.

"I feel like I'm glowing," Elle responded.

Elle actually was glowing, from the inside out, it was coming from inside her womb, a gentle force was growing.

"I feel so alive, so... present, so... as if I'm more than this. Do you know what I mean?" Elle continued.

"Oh yes," Agnes replied, "I wish I was young as you again, hm, young love."

Elle took Agnes's hand, they looked each other in the eye. Agnes sighed, Elle gently squeezed her hand. At the corner of the street the agent looked up, sighed, and walked on. A few minutes passed, and the agent returned. He walked up to the terrace where Elle and Agnes were sitting and took a seat right next to them. He looked at Agnes and gently nodded. Then he slightly bent over towards them.

"Hello ladies, you don't know me, but I'm here to tell you that you should be aware of a friend of yours, Eddie, he's not who you think he is, and he's actually quite dangerous."

Before Elle or Agnes could respond the agent already stood up and left.

"What the...," Agnes said.

They looked at each other and then in the direction to where the agent left. He was gone alright. They looked at each other again.

"I think I'll have to talk to Eddie," Agnes said.

"Yeah, me too," Elle responded.

Twenty-five

"Hi mum!" Marie-Isobelle says.

"Hello daughter!" Françoise replies.

"Good afternoon darling wife!" I join in.

"Hello darling husband!" Françoise replies.

"Mai and I already prepared for dinner. How long for Eddie to be here?"

"He said he'd be here in twenty-thirty minutes."

"A drink before that?"

"Yes please!"

After Eddie arrives they have a lively discussion about astrophysics, Marie-Isobelle's major.

"The event horizon of the black hole," Marie-Isobelle says, "is where matter and existence speed up and transform into another dimension. Because of its intensity, the compacting energy that is involved, it actually lights up, it emits light that we can see from Earth."

"Yup," Eddie responds, "it's actually quite dramatic, because that is the moment, the phase in time and space, where all the information that is being pulled into the black hole is seen for the last time. It would be the last moment anything could be saved in our dimensions."

Françoise and I enjoy watching how Marie-Isobelle is glowing with enthusiasm, not just physically, but because she loves it so much. We enjoy how she's able to talk about it, discuss it, explore it.

"What do you think about the Mantle theory?" she then asks Eddie. Because she noticed the question marks in our eyes, she starts to explain.

"The Mantle theory says that outside our Multiverse there is a similar black mantle, that pulls our Multiverse outward, into this other dimension where a new parallel, or semi-parallel existence is formed."

"I think it sounds credible," Eddie replies.

"Oh, wait," Marie-Isobelle continues with a smile, "there's more! The black mantle is connected with the black holes. The black-hole-mantle entity is somewhat like a mix of a torus and a Klein bottle. That's it."

She concludes with a somewhat theatrical wave of her arm.

I give her a round of applause and both Françoise and Eddie join in.

"Well yes," Eddie says, "like I said, it's credible, and, well, that's what we have young ladies like you for, to find out, right? Since the early twenty-first century there is a similar discussion about the information you mentioned, either being lost into the black hole, or actually lingering on the rim, the event horizon."

Marie-Isobelle listens, and seems to think about it. Then Françoise joins in.

"How do you think this relates to time travel?" while she looks at Eddie.

"Have you ever time-travelled?" he asks her.

"Yes I did, it made me very sick, I don't think it's really for me."

"No, no, never, I don't think I'm made for that," I say when Eddie looks at me. "Ah well, maybe not yet."

Marie-Isobelle starts glowing again.

"I think I could, or, can I?" she asks when looking at Françoise and me.

"I think your mother knows more about that than I do," I say to her.

"I think she's more capable than me, so yes, I think you safely could."

Eddie folds both his hands under his chin.

"If you're sure, I could show you? If your parents agree?"

"Her parents know she's old enough to decide herself, right?" I say. "But I'm OK with it if your mother is also OK with it?"

"Operation Kodaira," Françoise says.

We all look at her with question marks in our eyes.

"Yes, OK, if it's one hundred percent safe. Eddie?"

"It's one hundred percent safe. Otherwise I wouldn't be here, right?" he replies with a smile, knowing what only he knows, about his recent transformation, without the Transformer.

"We'll use my Transformer," he continues, "I can vow for it to be perfectly safe. You know the way it works has been described like a controlled, inside-out black hole bubble?"

"That's supposed to make it feel safer?" Marie-Isobelle asks with a smile.

"Hm, maybe not, but I can prove it to you, if you want?"

Marie-Isobelle gives it a little thought.

"Bring me a small object from the past, that doesn't disturb time, and then bring it back."

"I can do that," Eddie replies, "you want that now?"

A little later they are all outside the house, and Eddie creates a bubble with the Transformer, a few moments later he's gone, leaving the family waiting in excitement. A few more moments later, the bubble returns and Eddie stands covered in dirt and something in his hand.

"I'm sorry, I had to get myself dirty to avoid standing out too much." He then stretches out his arm and shows... a brick.

"Let's see if you can guess where this is coming from," he then says.

"Amsterdam," I say, as it looks like the red bricks on the canals of Amsterdam.

"Nope, but not bad at all."

"Oh, New York, Paris, it could be from anywhere," Françoise says.

"Well yes, and no. You see, from the same period there are bricks in many cities around the world. But there's something specific about this brick," while he hands the brick to Marie-Isobelle.

"EH," she says, reading the two characters on the back of the brick.

"Eduard Hubert," Françoise says.

"Edouard Hubert," Eddie says, while performing a gentle bow towards her.

"OK, then what is this about?" I ask him.

"I've been a master brickmaker in France, those are my initials indeed," while he looks at Françoise. "I've worked for a little while on the Palace of Versailles, to blend in, and be close to the centre of affairs in France. As a master brickmaker I could get where I needed to be. I can take you while we bring back the brick? It won't take long," he then asks Marie-Isobelle.

After a little while Marie-Isobelle and Eddie are in late 17th century France, about 1671, as it is still not an exact proficiency, more a skill that gets better with experience, and while Marie-Isobelle is introduced as his visiting niece, they walk towards a place with large amounts of wet bricks, prepared to be fired.

"You see, my initials," he says. Marie-Isobelle looks at it with a smile.

"Unbelievable!" she says.

"Oh wait," he then says, "if we turn it like this, we'll have your initials, MI." They both laugh while Eddie takes the stamp from a brick worker and turns it slightly around showing what indeed looks like an M and an I, on top of each other.

"Vanity was a thing already in this time, wasn't it?" Marie-Isobelle asks.

"It's not just vanity," Eddies replies with a smile, "it's also for the proper payments. As you can see there are many brickmakers here, and with the stamp we all get paid for what we've produced. That's fair, isn't it? And I don't stand out too much, at least not in a way that would alter our time, ah well, your time, my time. Well, at least not with the bricks."

They walk along the production field, and behind those they watch the Palace of Versailles, taking shape into the famous buildings of Louis XIV, *"le Roi Soleil"*. High above them, a Sentinel watches over them.

"That wasn't too bad, was it?" Eddie asks Marie-Isobelle after they've returned to her parents' house.

"Haven't we altered time with the dirt on our shoes?"

"Time is more flexible, more healing, than most people actually still believe it is," Eddie replies.

Françoise and I walk towards them.

"That took a bit longer than I expected," I say, "I was actually getting a bit worried."

Marie-Isobelle runs towards us, and with a big hug starts to tell about her little big adventure.

"It was unbelievable," she says, "I've seen the palace of the French king being built, and Eddie showed me where the brick with his initials came from. Unbelievable! Beautiful!"

After they both carefully wash their hands, they sit at the dinner table.

"You know you'll have to sterilise your shoes, don't you?" Eddie asks.

"Yeah, of course," Marie-Isobelle says.

"How come this works for you? Without interrupting time," she then asks Eddie.

"It works because most construction workers travel," he explains, "I can come and go, as I can travel on when it suits me."

"Makes sense," I say while I watch Marie-Isobelle still being very happy with the experience.

"I felt different," she says, "as if I wasn't the same person that I am now."

"That should be correct," Françoise says, "the properties of your person belong to this time. Here you are who you are now. There you are who you'd be then, if that makes sense?"

"In a way? I guess?" She pauses for a moment. "He introduced me as his niece, in fluent French! If I'd travel there again, do I still have to introduce myself as your niece?"

"Depends, if you'd travel to the same time and place, that would be the preferred option. Continuity is still the preferred option," Eddie says. "There cannot be too many time travellers at the same time though. Imagine if everyone would start time-travelling, it would completely mess up our past, and with that our present and future. What we did could be done because it's interchangeable with several of the many other brickmakers, but then again even too much of very little can be harmful. You know what I mean?"

Marie-Isobelle nods, while taking a bite. I notice she starts glowing again.

"My tongue feels weird," she says.

It's not just her tongue though, it looks as if her lips are getting the same colour as her tongue. Françoise notices too.

"Can you show me your tongue Mai?" Françoise asks.

"Sure," and she swallows the last bit of her bite.

Françoise looks at a slightly glowing tongue and matching lips. For a moment she's silent, thinking of it.

"You're already completing the sequence," she says, "you're becoming who you can be. After becoming who you are, you're becoming who you can be."

We all look at Françoise, at Marie-Isobelle, and back.

"It's good, it's good!" Françoise says, "It's beautiful!"

Marie-Isobelle quickly walks from the table to grab a mirror.

"Wait till I tell Chisato!"

Twenty-six

Eddie was nowhere to be seen for the next few days. Somehow something else was keeping him busy. He had noticed indeed that time was speeding up, but it was not linear, not logarithmic. Eventually he concluded it was in waves. And not all time-dimensions shared the same pattern, it somehow seemed as if one line he was living was catching up with the other, a synchronisation of some sort. With his new added form, as a Sentinel, he travelled back to Versailles, he found peace amongst the business of the construction of the new palace. Sometimes seemingly as a human, sometimes as a light orb, a Sentinel.

"Most humans still do not realise the uniqueness of existence on Earth," he said to himself. "Earth, with its unique limitations, offers unique opportunities for learning, which cannot be learned or experienced elsewhere in this Multiverse."

In the realm of Sentinels though, awareness was of a different order, a lot of things didn't matter, while other things emerged from new, existential perspectives. Eddie quickly adapted to his new form, where communication between Sentinels was of a different order. Why and how wasn't entirely clear to him, though he felt more and more that indeed the confrontation at the boundary of his existence and the dark agent, would have triggered it. While Sentinels appeared to be the same, each one had a different vibration, a different tone, a different voice, if you could call it like that.

Joan didn't like Decembers, and actually neither did I. The Christmas meetings, the superficial social town show celebrations, they all seemed so childish, so not of this world, so not of our world, so just for the purpose of consumerism, profits, and politics. We didn't understand why humanity had still not grown up. But then again, the children seemed to enjoy it. This year in Strasbourg, the Christmas tree seemed to be bigger than ever, so much so, that I thought it could be, or should be, a fake one. But it was hard to tell as the public was not allowed to come close to it. Probably they didn't want a huge fire like last year. Considering Joan's pregnancy we both ordered a mild green tea, from our favourite little cafe.

In Amsterdam Elle's pregnancy was making it impossible for her to safely use her bicycle, as that was her favourite way to tour the city. Instead Elle and Françoise made short strolls along the canals, as long as it wasn't slippery though. There was love and care around them, Françoise felt as if it was also her child, of course she did. Elle felt the same. Eddie came by to visit them, and to show them his new tattoo: "$E = mc^2$".

"Matter into energy and energy into matter," he said.

"Does it matter?" Elle asked laughing.

"It matters to me," he said. "It matters to all of us! Especially to you," while looking at Elle.

Françoise just watched, amused to see where this was going.

"OK," he continued, "because you asked for it. What do you think of time travel, or interdimensional travel?"

"OK, where have you been? What have you been smoking?" Françoise asked.

Eddie paused for a moment.

"I can't tell you," he said.

"Here, have a drink, and then you can tell us," Elle said.

Françoise was having a hard time not laughing out loud, as she tried to stay serious.

"What do you think of parallel interdimensional time

travel?" Eddie continued.

"What are you trying to say, Eddie?" Françoise finally asked.

"What if I told you I can't tell you?" Eddie said again. "Or can I?"

He didn't, instead he just told about "the Five Second Constant", the method of measuring time speeding up. And they just talked about Elle's baby, how it would grow up in such a different world, how it would grow up as such a different being. Seemingly not knowing what they were really talking about, or did they?

"You know what?" Elle then said, "I think you know shit. I think you're just guessing what it could be like, making it seem interesting, making yourself seem interesting, I don't know. Do you?"

There was a silence for a few moments. Then Françoise started laughing out loud.

"Where did that come from?" she asked.

A few more moments of silence followed.

"Must be those hormones," Eddie said, while ducking away.

Elle raised a fist at Eddie, but she smiled with it.

Elle had touched a nerve, Eddie indeed was trying to say

something that he wasn't comfortable with. Not comfortable with what he was trying to say, and not comfortable with how to say it, or even if to say it at all. Not only Elle was touched by changing hormones, Eddie also was changing and wasn't entirely comfortable with it. Elle decided not to talk about the little incident with the agent, she felt Eddie was alright.

When Joan and I returned to our car I helped her into it, for its low-positioned seats. Maybe my car wasn't the best choice at this stage anymore. I got in and a car parked beside us, beside me, and the driver stepped out with a huge smile on his face. He walked up to me and said he had never seen one for real. Then he kneeled down and showed pictures of his classic Fiat Abarth.

"When you see this white one driving, you'll know it's me," he said, smiling.

Even though I was somewhat on alert, the feeling of a *déjà vu*, I felt he was genuinely being enthusiastic, and Joan felt the same. He went on to his doctor's appointment, and we drove off, home. Although the roads generally were smooth, with every little bump I looked to the side if Joan was alright. Of course she was alright, but when we arrived home I decided it was the last time during this pregnancy we'd be driving the 4C together.

"It was fun," she said, and then she stumbled or slipped, and fell to her knees. I wasn't sure, but I thought I saw a moment of glow coming from her belly. Too short to be sure, but my main concern was with Joan and the baby. The muscles around her belly had tightened, a natural reflex, protection increased. The next morning we'd visit the hospital to check if everything was still alright.

And it was. I kept thinking though, about that moment where it seemed as if I saw Joan's belly light up, glow. Joan said she felt her muscles tighten, as they still were tightened, on alert. But they would start to relax soon, the doctor had said.

Someone was watching, and it wasn't Eddie, nor was it the Sentinel.

In Amsterdam, Elle and Françoise could feel the baby becoming more and more communicative, but they also felt as if someone, or something was around them that shouldn't be there. There was some kind of pressure, that wasn't physical, nor mental, that sometimes made them feel uncomfortable, uneasy. On the one hand they felt joy, and on the other hand they felt like being on alert. Together though, they felt strong, very strong. Slowly the day was coming where they expected the baby to be born. Slowly but surely Elle and Françoise were getting ready. Surely the house was ready, but they didn't yet know if it was for a boy or a girl. They didn't yet want to know. They wanted to enjoy the surprise of life to the max. I didn't know, but surely started to feel its presence more and more. A week before Christmas I felt like I should visit them. Joan was feeling alright again, so I went. This time though, as the weather was getting worse, I went by train.

On the train, I realised I should have gone by car. The zombies, or semi-AI, as I often thought of them, hooked on to the machine, leaving their humanity at home, made me feel more from home than I actually was. I tried to relax, and then I simply fell asleep.

In Amsterdam, Françoise was waiting at the door, she looked beautiful, warm, generous. She gave me a warm hug, and for a moment I could feel the first day we met before in Amsterdam, and I'm sure she did too.

Elle was sitting relaxed in the sitting room, reading a book, I guess.

"So, finally," she said.

I walked up to her, and she gave me a kiss, looked me deep in the eyes, and then said "finally" again. I wasn't sure what to think of that, but also wasn't too sure how to respond as I didn't want to jump into a discussion right after I had entered the room. She felt warm though, and while Françoise walked to the kitchen to get us some tea, Elle looked at me, with her warm lips, gentle smile, her beautiful, big open eyes and her babyful belly.

"Do you want to feel it?" she asked.

"Yes, sure."

I walked up to her, and rubbed my hands as I didn't want the winter cold to disturb her, and the baby. Elle was wearing a thin shirt, so it felt as if I was touching her skin. There was a small shudder, and I felt as if I saw that glow again. Elle looked at me and said, "It's OK. You can kiss it if you want."

I kissed her belly, and the baby responded. I kissed her again, and again the baby responded.

"She pushed back. Did you feel that?" I asked Elle.

"Yes, " she said, "she loves to push back. Oh wait, we're calling the baby a she now?"

While Françoise came back in the room, Elle and I were

looking at each other, and question marks were dancing around in the room.

"What is that about?" Françoise asked.

"I felt the baby is a girl," I said.

"And we don't even know," Elle said smiling.

Françoise looked at me again, smiling.

"He knows," she said, "he knows."

From that moment on the baby was a girl. Or a boy, as I wasn't sure whether or not I was projecting Joan's sense onto Elle's baby.

"I'm sorry," she said, when she looked me deep in my eyes.

"I am sorry," I said.

She stood up and gave me a hug.

"Group hug!" Françoise said a few moments later.

All three of us had tears in our eyes, not just because we were sorry, but also out of happiness, I thought. They were beautiful. They were more than beautiful, they were glowing with beauty.

While I went home the next day, Eddie stayed close. Eddie knew something no-one of us knew, but might soon find out.

After Elle had visited her doctor in the morning, she came home with a message that was somewhat alarming. Not for me though, as I only learned about it later. Her doctor had advised her to have the baby sooner rather than later, a caesarean was planned for the next day.

When the baby was born, the doctors were quite surprised. Not so much with the baby, beautiful and healthy, but with Elle. Never before had they seen this muscle structure. Never had they seen before, as Eddie knew and understood very well, what he referred to as a biological robot. And to be clear, not just Elle, but also Françoise…

Twenty-seven

The Artificial Intelligence community worries me. If they learn about Marie-Isobelle's changes they will feel threatened, and all for good reason, as they are. While their numbers already were falling, but quite steady now, for all the different variations, I just learned that their numbers are actually now falling again, especially the ones with more advanced technology. The other way around than one would have expected. Well, I think MODUs have been accepted as the new norm for a while now? Yeah.

Chisato and Marie-Isobelle are having a cup of tea in the the shade of the afternoon sun. While Marie-Isobelle takes a bite of her cherry cake, she looks at Chisato. She licks her lips and removes the cream from it. Then she licks her lips again. And again, and Chisato begins to laugh.

"Yes, I believe your cake is good!" she says.

Then Marie-Isobelle licks her lips again, with a gentle smile.

"That's not it," she says.

"Oh wait, you're wearing lipstick!" Chisato then responds.

"Almost there."

Chisato comes a little bit closer to study Marie-Isobelle's face, her mouth, her lips. Marie-Isobelle sticks out her tongue, a little bit, and moves it from left to right over her lips.

"Oh no!" Chisato says surprised. "Oh no!"

"Oh yes," Marie-Isobelle replies.

"Oh no."

"Oh yes."

Then it's quiet for a few seconds.

"My father told about this, it's true. It is you!"

Chisato leans forward again.

"Show me again?"

Marie-Isobelle sticks out her tongue, not too much, just enough.

"Oooh, they are the same, they are the same," Chisato says. "If you wouldn't know, you wouldn't see it," she continues, "it's beautiful."

She moves forward to give Marie-Isobelle a quick kiss on her lips, Marie-Isobelle responds with a warm hug.

Chisato sticks out her tongue.

"What about me?" she asks.

"Your tongue is still the same colour as mine, your lips seem the same as they were before."

"I want your lips," Chisato says, with a smile.

"Here," and Marie-Isobelle gives her a kiss on her lips.

They both blush, smile and then sit back in their chairs.

Marie-Isobelle looks at Chisato, and Chisato looks at Marie-Isobelle. For a few moments they hold each other's hands.

"Wow," Chisato says with a sigh.

Marie-Isobelle just smiles, and looks in the distance, thinking of her newly found appearance.

"It comes with benefits," she then says, "or maybe it's the other way around, I actually don't know."

If the Sentinel could smile, you could also see it smiling.

"You know," Marie-Isobelle continues, "I've changed. Well yes, of course I've changed, we just saw that, but it looks like slowly it seems like I can do other stuff, I can see other stuff. I can make more..., things, happen."

She sticks out her tongue and gently makes it glow. It looks as if her lips also slightly start to glow. And then it stops.

"When I do that," she says, "I also seem to see a different dimension, I see people in a different state, not much, but different. And with some people I can see, I can feel, other things. Like communication in a different way."

Chisato and Marie-Isobelle look each other straight in the eyes.

"Can you feel it?" Marie-Isobelle asks.

"I think, I think it is different, yes."

"My mother, and a friend from the institute where she works, explained to me how this is a changing phase, how it will give me access to a different level of energy."

"My father told about something like that," Chisato responds, "he said people like you would exist, with a growing inner access to a different kind of energy. He thought I could be one of them, but I'm not. You are."

For a moment she sits back, seemingly disappointed.

"I changed," Marie-Isobelle then says, "maybe you can change too?"

Chisato sits right up.

"Yes, that would be great! My father said we could change the world!"

Almost like two children with new toys, they marvel in their newly found world, a new territory, a newly found form of awareness.

A flash appears. It bounces off Marie-Isobelle. Chisato ducks away. The flash forms into a streaming form that seems to try to encapsulate Marie-Isobelle, but she fights it off. Within a few seconds the streaming energy form lets go and disappears.

"Did you see where that came from?" Marie-Isobelle asks.

"No," Chisato says, with her eyes now wide open. "What was that?"

They both look around them, nobody seemed to have noticed. Nobody seems to know. But the agent knows and Eddie wasn't near. On alert, Marie-Isobelle tries to come to grips with the situation.

"I think it tried to somehow grab me," she says, "I felt it pulling me out of here, out of here and now. But it didn't happen, I think I'm stronger now, or different. More than what it, or they expected, I guess?"

She now thinks about Eddie, and the way time travel could also be done in different ways, for all kinds of purposes. Chisato talks to her, but she doesn't hear it.

"Mai, Mai, are you alright?"

"Yeah, yeah. Everything is changing so quickly, I don't

get it. Why?"

The Sentinel goes back to some kind of stasis, recovering from the action. She was there at the right moment, at the right place, to protect Marie-Isobelle.

The agent is gone, he now knows he won't be able to get Marie-Isobelle as easy as he thought it would be. But then again, who was he kidding?

Marie-Isobelle finishes her tea.

"Let's go," Marie-Isobelle says.

"Wait."

"What? Oh, sorry."

Chisato takes another sip from her tea.

"Why are we leaving now?"

Marie-Isobelle doesn't answer.

"Everything seems OK, doesn't it?"

Chisato feels the presence of the Sentinel, and slowly Marie-Isobelle comes to feel it too, as she starts to relax, a bit.

"I'll have another tea, please," she says, looks up and as a gesture of gratitude tips with her index finger against her head. They have contact. It's warm, they both have a pulsating glow. The waitress thought she saw something, but isn't sure. Chisato sees it, smiles at Marie-Isobelle and takes another sip from her tea.

"You know," Marie-Isobelle says, "there's more to this. Things are changing so fast, and at the same time, time doesn't seem to be what it, ehm, seems to be. I don't seem to be who I thought I was. How about you?"

"Well, I read most of my father's reports, and we discussed a lot about it. When he was still alive."

Chisato pauses for a moment, a group of loud students pass by, followed by their teacher. The teacher looks at Marie-Isobelle, they have eye contact. She feels a buzz, she feels as if there was some kind of deeper, bigger contact, some kind of communication.

"I feel," Chisato continues, "as if my father knew something about this world, already before he started his research, that relates to what we are experiencing now. Something that is more, deeper, bigger, than what we've all thought it was."

Twenty-eight

A baby was born. Another baby was born. With the Christmas festivities finally behind us, the baby chose calmer waters to come into this world. Joan was feeling great, and the baby was too. A great, wonderful little baby girl.

"I'd like to name her after my grandmother," Joan said, "after all, because of her we both met, right?"

"Ehm, remind me again, oh wait, wasn't her name Marie-Isobelle? A bit traditional, isn't it?"

"Well, you can have all kinds of modern, sparkling nick-names as a variation of it? Ehm, how about Mai? Mai, dinner is ready! Mai, did you clean up your room? Sounds OK, doesn't it?"

I couldn't really argue with that, so after a few more days of talks and negotiations Marie-Isobelle it was. After all, when she was seventeen she could change her name if she wanted to. But then again, why would she? I started to feel comfortable with it, I actually did like the sound of it. And in short form, it was amusing too. Mai was born in January. Funny, sort of.

I felt energetic, inspired, I felt like painting again. And so I did. I visited the Strasbourg ArtS Academy and discussed using one of their ateliers. I didn't get one, but one of the masters students, an exchange student from California, allowed me to share his room with him, after all he had the largest room in the building.

After a week he said he didn't have enough money to continue his projects, and asked me if he could make a painting for me in exchange for funding paint and brushes for him. I discussed it with Joan, and then I took him to an artists' shop, where he bought a large amount of paint and brushes. Well, I bought them for him, and he could continue working, including on a painting for Joan and me. He first thought of making a variation of "American Gothic", but I thought that had been done so often already. I thought I'd leave him to come up with another idea, while I started working on my own new projects. Joan, and especially Mai were great inspirations. I wanted to make a reflection of our world for Mai, a reflection in time, a reflection of time, of her world. A reflection and an exploration.

I tried, but didn't get a thing on the canvas, somehow too many different issues were competing in my mind. So I spent more time at home, getting to know our Mai, and helping Joan. It felt good.

The beauty of life was becoming clearer to me. Through the eyes of Mai I learned to see differently. I felt that my open-mindedness was even becoming more open.

Françoise and I had a few talks over the phone, and she wrote another letter, as she felt that was more personal. She was back in Brussels for a few weeks, and felt closer to me. "So close and yet so far away," she said. Her feelings for me seemed endless, she talked about love, our love, which she said she doesn't do easily, yet she described our love, our conversation as light, easy, wonderful. Somehow however, there would always be a sense of reality, a reality where my marriage with Joan, and now also including Mai, made a normal, loving, caring relationship pretty complicated. We both felt though, that what was making it complicated was our sense of conventional relationships, even though so much already had changed, or had it? What is a normal relationship after all? What is love after all? It felt as if we were all stretching it as some kind of survival mechanism, trying to find a way, a new way, if there was one. Of course there was one!

When I held Mai I felt the epitome of unconditional love. It felt as if this beautiful, warm being was helping me to understand my own life, my own relationships, with Françoise, with Elle and also with Joan, with my own youth, with the world. What a beautiful world!

How long had I been sitting here, in this recliner, with Mai sleeping on my lap? Almost an hour.

"Hello, hello," I said softly while Mai slowly opened her eyes. "Hello Mai, did you sleep well?"

Joan came in. "Shall I take her from you? Then I can also feed her if she wants."

After sitting almost motionless for an hour I welcomed the suggestion, even though I found it almost therapeutical just to sit with a sleeping baby on my lap, in my arms.

I rose from the chair and give Mai to Joan.

A loud bang crashed in from outside, both Joan and I ducked away with Mai in between us, sheltering her from whatever was happening. One door had flung open and the cold rushed in. Then Eddie seemed to appear out of nowhere.

"Are you OK?" he asked.

"We are OK, are we?" I asked Joan.

We both looked at Mai who looked at us with big eyes, she cried from the sudden shock. We both kept her sheltered for a little longer, then Joan took her to the next room, while I walked out towards Eddie.

"It's clear," he said, "they want to hurt you and your little baby."

"Where did you come from? How did you know?" I asked him, while I studied the damage.

"I've been following him for a while now," Eddie said, "he tried to place some explosive material here, and I think I was just in time."

"Just in time?"

"Yes, this was only a small, relatively meaningless explosion. It was just part of the preparation. I think if I was here ten minutes later it would have been quite different."

"How, I don't know, what are you talking about?"

Eddie paused for a moment. That moment took too long for me and I went inside again to check on Mai and Joan. Mai was drinking with Joan, though. It looked so peaceful, as if nothing had happened. Joan felt the same, she smiled.

I went back outside and saw Eddie checking the roof. There was very little damage compared to the noise.

"Lucky," Eddie said.

"Yeah, lucky?"

We tried if we could close the door again, and with some shoving and pushing the lock clicked in place again. We'd have it replaced within the next few days, of course.

"I think you need to know," Eddie said, "this guy is out to get you, but it's enough now, and I'll be on his heels to make sure this doesn't happen again."

"So, are you a cop after all? Some kind of secret service?"

"Some people think I'm kind of, you know," Eddie looks thoughtful, "well, I think you could say that alright."

He looked me straight in the eyes. He was either trying to be honest, or an immensely talented actor.

"Well then, who is he? What does he want? Why, why did he do this? Do you know?"

This was when Eddie sat down with me, and for the first time really started to talk, whether I believed it or not, it seemed.

"OK, he said, "you've been part of this for a while already, you might as well know. Nothing happens by accident. You stood out quite a while ago. You thought you didn't, but you did. We had been looking for you for quite a while. Why, you may ask. Because a well-known researcher found a connection between the talents of seeing colours and a higher form of awareness. This higher form of awareness has proven to be the key, the portal towards opening the human mind into higher dimensions."

I listen to him without saying a word, focusing, trying to be aware of everything he says. So much so that for a few moments I completely forgot where I was, and what had just happened.

"You may remember professor Kodaira," he then continued, "he was the trigger to this all. He found you, and made us aware of you. We think you could be the key."

I started to feel very uncomfortable and at the same time I felt some kind of pride.

"It makes sense, and it doesn't," I said.

"Elle and Françoise," he said, "are not who you think they are. Well, not exactly. They don't even know themselves, but I've noticed they're starting to figure it out. Elle and Françoise, as beautiful, as smart, as kind as they may seem, are not normal humans. They both have been part of a research project to enhance human beings. When Artificial Intelligence robots started to become corruptible, and started to get corrupted in unprecedented ways, the need for other ways to enhance humanity was explored, and Elle and Françoise were part of that. Some refer to them as biological robots, but I think that's quite a disservice to them. I think they still are humans, but with the unique gift of reproducing your specific higher, human awareness.

Sadly Françoise lost her baby, and we still do not really understand why, even though she might have been exposed to some form of targeted, damaging, destructive force or radiation."

I was listening, but at the same time my imagination took a hold of me, and I felt a deep, caring sadness towards Françoise. Eddie seemed to notice.

"It wasn't your fault," he said. "If anyone was to blame, you could blame us, I suppose. But then again, we didn't try to harm you, or Françoise. On the other hand, it seems Elle and her baby are doing perfectly alright, and they are happy. Even Françoise is happy with them. You know they, Elle and Françoise share a higher consciousness?"

"No, no, but then again, after all this, should I be surprised?"

The door opened, and Joan came in. Mai was asleep in her arms.

"I'll bring her in her bed so she can sleep quietly," she said.

"Ehm, wouldn't it be better if she stays here with us?" I asked, while looking at Joan and Eddie.

"Why?" Joan asked, "her room is quiet, warm and safe?"

Eddie nodded without saying a word.

"Of course," I said, "of course."

"I'll have another look around the house," Eddie said, "and then I'll leave you without my disturbance, if that's OK with you?"

"Sure."

"OK, have a great evening together. Do you want me to arrange for a repair man?"

"No, no, we'll be fine, thank you."

"If there is anything else, contact me! Cheerio!"

Twenty-nine

The weather is fine. Summer is fine, especially when the morning comes alive. I parked my car outside the garage and she's getting a nice polish. It feels very relaxing, and Françoise is watching me.

"I love you too!" she calls out, while making a stroking gesture with her hand. We both laugh and throw kisses. A little later she walks up to me and starts to talk about Eddie, and information she found in the institute's library.

"Eddie is involved deeper in the M-institute than I thought," she starts to explain, "he actually was there from the beginning. Yesterday he told me about early dimensional time travel where he was involved in the initial creation of superhumans. They didn't call it that then, but nevertheless. He was not directly responsible though, he's not a scientist, or a doctor for that matter. It is more like being a part in its organisation, well, that's how he explained it."

For a moment I stop with the car, and look at Françoise, as she is standing there with two cups of tea.

"Oh sorry," she says, "I brought some."

Now I have to stop, and listen.

"He refers to it as parallel time travel, which he uses his Transformer for, but, he said, there are also other ways, of which he also mentioned the Sentinel. There are different Sentinels he said, different forms, and different individuals. Different individuals, from different times, good ones and bad ones. The bad ones, actually a bad group, he said, he was dealing with now."

She takes a sip from her tea, and sits down on the little stone wall close to me, suggesting I'd come sit with her, and I do.

"The bad ones, Eddie said, want to ruin, destroy our global society, they want to make such a mess that they believe they can provoke what they believe would be a second coming of Jesus. They are such selfish beings who do exactly the opposite of what they claim to believe in, and they do not see that. It's the opposite of love, and that's why they are trying to stop the slow but steady evolution of mankind into smarter, more caring, more aware beings. Instead of making life on Earth better, they want to make it worse."

"Mai," I say.

"Yes Mai, but Eddie believes she's already strong

enough."

For a moment it's silent, we both are thinking.

"Shouldn't we tell Mai?"

"Of course," Françoise replies.

As if we'd been calling her, Marie-Isobelle steps outside and walks towards us.

"Hey, being cosy without me?" she says, smiling. When she gets closer, she slows down and stops right in front of us. Then turns and wriggles her behind between us.

"That's better," she says, leaving us no room but to give in while trying to save our teas.

"We were actually having a serious talk," says Françoise, trying to keep a serious face, but she can't and bursts out laughing.

"Come on Mai, see what you're doing to your mother!"

"Yes? So what?" she replies, smiling.

"So wha-at?" Françoise returns.

Marie-Isobelle replies with a smug face, almost hiding a smile, and Françoise copies her. Marie-Isobelle leans back, but there's nothing to lean against, she almost falls. In a reflex she grabs my arm, the one where I was holding my tea, and the tea flies into the air and mostly gets spoiled over her. She makes some noises and slowly falls back onto the grass. There she is lying, on her back, feet on the wall. The next moment her whole body shudders with laughter.

Françoise isn't sure whether she should pull Marie-Isobelle back up, or slide down the wall to lay beside her. She slides down. I watch them both laying side by side, looking each other in the eyes.

"I love you mum."

"I love you too darling."

"I love you too dad! Come lay down with us!"

I wait a few seconds.

"OK."

I put away my empty tea cup, and slowly let myself slide down from the side of the little stone wall. And then we are lying there side by side.

"And now what?" I say.

"Family hug!" Marie-Isobelle says, while she tries to get her arms under both Françoise's neck and mine. We're all too busy to notice that high above, straight above us, a Sentinel is watching.

Later that day we try to pick up our conversation.

"Your mother had a long talk with Eddie yesterday, and that's what we were just talking about."

Marie-Isobelle gives me an enquiring look, and waits for me to continue. I give her the short version of what we talked about, and then Françoise raises her hand.

"Well yes" she says, "but that's only where we left off. Our issue is where it touches on you, Mai. How it matters for you. Do you understand?"

The conversation that follows leaves no doubt that Marie-Isobelle is well aware of the situation, and somehow is very confident in how she can handle it. Finally Françoise and I look each other in the eyes, also confident that she'll be right.

"In a way," she says, "they both are doing what they think, or believe is right. Eddie wants to protect life on Earth for the future of humanity, and that dark agent, or his organisation wants to ruin it to provoke something like a second coming that they believe in."

"Well yes, that's about it," I say.

"Good versus bad, but then reversed," Marie-Isobelle concludes.

"That's a fascinating way of putting it," Françoise concludes.

The next morning Marie-Isobelle looks in the mirror as

she is studying her tongue and lips.

"Mum!" she then calls.

Her mum comes into the bathroom.

"Why are my tongue, and lips, different from yours? Different from dad's?"

Now they both stand in front of the mirror, both sticking out their tongues. Françoise's fascinating turquoise, and Marie-Isobelle's deep, warm purple. They both start laughing.

"Your dad's a Natural," she says, "I'm a hybrid, as they say, and you are our product." She acts very serious, which confuses Marie-Isobelle. But then she starts smiling again. "You are the best of us," Françoise continues, "the best, most beautiful, most wonderful being on this planet!"

She gives Marie-Isobelle a kiss and watches if she's alright.

"OK," Marie-Isobelle responds, "I'll finish my packing and then I'll be on my way again."

"OK, I'll be outside if you need anything."

Later in the afternoon Marie-Isobelle is in Amsterdam again. With her backpack on she walks to her apartment. Along the way she watches people's faces, their eyes, their lips, possibly their tongues? Which lips are real? Which are make-up? A few people give her strange looks back, but every now and then it feels good. And then it hits her, locked onto the eyes of a passer-by. She shakes her head, as it feels uncomfortable, as if she's being read on the inside. But then she realises she also saw the other person's inside. She turns around but the guy walks on. Marie-Isobelle decides to do the same. She passes groups of tourists, locals having an afternoon beer, and more tourists. Somewhat on alert, she keeps studying faces and wishes people wouldn't be wearing make-up. It would make life so much easier, she thinks. Nobody watches up. Marie-Isobelle arrives at her apartment.

I look at the clock on my desk, and the time it mentions ends on 2 minutes and 58 seconds. For no specific reason I look at the clock again, about half a minute later, and it says 3 minutes and 4 seconds. I keep watching for about five seconds, then let it go. I'm not sure if it relates to my episodes of memory loss, but then again, this is the other way around.

Marie-Isobelle calls, just to say she is back in Amsterdam and she is alright.

"I wish you were here," she says, but doesn't explain why.

"We'll see you next weekend," I say, trying to be cheerful, a good father.

Eddie is on alert. Instead of him watching the agent, the agent now seems to be watching him. Eddie has been back to his own time and learned more about the agent. In fact the agent is not a representative of the religious fanatics, but he has a self-interest in the destruction of Earth. Total mining of any and all of its materials, exploitation of its energy and the humans doing it for him. He's been doing it since ages, Eddie learned. The Armageddon fanatics believe they get what they want, and the exploiters surely get what they want. At the M-institute, Eddie and Françoise are discussing the situation, in her office.

"What do you think we should do?" Françoise asks.

"Well, I have a tag on him, so I know where he is. And he's following me. In fact that's an easy way for me to keep an eye on him, isn't it?"

"Yeah, so probably we should be more alert when he's not following you then?"

"Yeah," Eddie says with a somewhat nervous smile.

"You know they cloned our babies?" Eddie then says seemingly out of the blue.

Françoise looks at him with big question marks in her eyes.

"Cloned our babies?" she repeats. "When? What for?"

"They tried to make biological robots, soulless biological robots. But it didn't work out. Pretty brutal, right?"

"When did that happen?"

"Oh, some fifty, sixty years ago. But as I said, it didn't work for them as they thought it would. Just to say they're into anything if they believe it furthers their cause."

"Yup, history repeats when humans do not learn," Françoise says.

"In fact, it not just repeats, it also gets worse," Eddie adds.

"But then, it always gets worse, before it gets better!" Françoise then says.

Later that day, in the archives of the M-institute Françoise is reading up on old files and finds Eddie has been active around the M-institute on more projects than she thought. Von Neumann probes, Professor Hikari Kodaira, Operation OK, they all already are in the oldest files, and as such have been involved since a very long time. The biological experiments also are older than she thought they were. At some point, if even just for a moment, she considers that even her husband could be some kind of a biological robot.

"Or is he?" she thinks. "Hacked? Recovered?"

"Me, a biological robot? Really? Come on! In your dreams," I say.

Thirty

It was dark, we had dinner together. Elle asked if I would like to have a walk outside with her. I had left my coat in the car, so she gave me one of hers, the widest one she had. It would do for a not too long walk. So, we were walking outside in the snow. We were talking, strolling along with each other. We were having fun. Arm in arm, close together, cosy and warm. When we approached some bushes, full of snow, I gave her a small, teasing push, towards the bushes. Just teasing, nothing more. "You can do that with your wife," she said. I was confused, why did she say that? Was she talking about making love? And then I woke up.

In the cold of February Françoise had travelled back to Brussels, she wrote in her letter, to work on and discuss her research project. "So close and yet so far away," she wrote. Sometimes I wondered why she wrote these wonderful, unbelievably warm and caring, handwritten letters, as if she was waiting for something. Waiting for something to change? Waiting for me to change?

I didn't want to change, I wanted to grow, I wanted to

grow beyond who I was, I wanted to grow beyond myself. I wanted to give my love to my dearest ones, all the love they deserved, and they deserved all my love. And in between it all, there was Mai, the dearest one of all.

Mai was a happy child, with an enquiring mind, she loved to touch my face with both hands. I loved being with her, communicating with her, she made me see things differently. I was a happy father, for sure.

I wasn't sure about Françoise anymore. Was she still a happy traveller?

Eddie and the time-travelling agent met once more, both keeping a safe distance from each other. This was not a fight, then what was it? Eddie was for Operation Kodaira, the agent was against it.

"In my future it leads to this."

"In my future it leads to that."

They both could visualise their thoughts onto each other. Both seemingly trying to win the other over with arguments that neither would accept. For a moment Eddie thought he should end the issue while he could, there and then. But it seemed the agent saw it coming, and said goodbye.

"See you later alligator," Eddie responded.

Eddie decided to go back to Versailles. He loved the simple way of life surrounding him there, and then. Everything seemed so straightforward, even the crooks, he thought. He had seen the waste of time and money with parts of the palace being built and then destroyed because the king had changed his mind. In a way it was quite amusing, he thought. But when he tried to morph into a Sentinel form, it didn't work anymore. No matter how he tried, it didn't work anymore. Why? He didn't know. Was it something temporary? Was the last meeting with the agent related? He didn't know. He had to go back to his good old, reliable Transformer. He wanted to get out of it badly. He then wanted to go and see Paris. So, he went to see Paris, and saw the newly constructed *Avenue des Champs-Élysées*, referred to as *le Grand Promenade* then, more than one hundred and fifty years before the construction of the *Arc de Triomphe*. Eddie decided to go see that too.

At some point he started to think of leaving the whole future mess as what it was, this life seemed so much more real, more profound, but he didn't, actually he couldn't. Even going far, far back wouldn't work, as time travel has its barriers, going forward Eddie couldn't get past his own time, and backward there was a barrier around the Medieval ages, the Dark Ages. Nobody knew why and there was no way to find out.

At the *Arc de Triomphe* it was 1939. Busy with cars and bicycles, and cafes offering packed chairs at small tables to watch the spectacle. He asked for a *grand crème*, even though he wasn't sure if he could stomach the old-fashioned dairy milk. But it turned out fine, he felt somewhat courageous because of it. He smiled, he realised how times would have changed.

Eddie enjoyed himself so much in the Paris of 1939 that he stayed for several weeks.

Elle had an appointment with him in Amsterdam a day later. What seemed like a month for Eddie, just was a day for Elle. Time didn't behave linearly, it behaved in waves. Almost as if it had a mind of its own.

"Hey Elle!"
"Hey Eddie!"

They hugged.

"How are you doing? And how's the little baby girl doing? Actually, what's her name?"

"Françoise and I had a few discussions about it. Françoise's actual name is Marie-Françoise, so we combined that with my first name. We decided on Maribelle."

Eddie was silent for a few moments.

"Are you sure?" he asked, as he realised there was another baby with almost the same name, from the same father. But then again he thought, who was he to meddle with that. They were all happy and healthy, and that was what seemed to matter the most.

"Where's Françoise?" Eddie asked.

"She's in Brussels, working on her research. She needs to gain some time as she was lagging behind. I feel for her. Françoise and I are some kind of twin sisters, we were supposed to live and enjoy life like normal people, but are we?"

"Maybe I should give her a visit too then?"

"I'm not sure Eddie, maybe she wants to be left alone for a while."

An hour later Eddie knocked on Françoise's door. She opened and was quite surprised.

"Eddie! What are you doing here?"

"I came to see how you're doing. Here, for you," and he gave her a colourful bouquet of roses.

"Oh, you didn't have to do that!"

"You deserve them, beautiful!"

She gave him a hug and invited him in.

"I hope I'm not interrupting?"

"Ah well, I needed a tea break anyhow. Want some too?"

"Yes please."

After a few minutes they were sitting with a cup of tea.

"Did you know they still served cow's milk in 1939?" he asked.

Françoise looked at him with suspicion.

"What is that?" she asked.

"You know, cow, milk, Paris, 1939?"

"You're funny," she said smiling.

"It's seriously true," he responded.

"No, I didn't know that. That's absurd, isn't it?"

"Yup, it really is. Should I show you?" he then asked.

"Show me what?"

"Paris, 1939."

"I know Paris 1939, it's part of my historic research, you know?"

"How about if I showed you real historic research? You know, real?"

"Are you offering to take me on a journey? I'm sorry, but I don't have time for that, and as a matter of fact I did most of my research travel already."

"How about I take a few hours from you and give you at least a day?"

Françoise put on a serious face and tried to determine what to make of Eddie's words.

"How? How would that work?"

Eddie looked at Françoise. He wanted to do something for her. He felt guilty for what happened to her, the baby, and that she had lost it. He wanted to give her something that would really make her happy.

"OK. Here goes."

He grabbed his bag and opened it.

"You can not talk about this with anybody," he said, "nobody, not even with Elle."

He put both hands in the bag, and took out the Transformer.

"What is that?"

Eddie softly put it on the table.

"That's the Transformer," he said, "like I said, you can

not talk about this with anybody, right?"

Françoise sighed.

"Right," she said.

"The Transformer," he said again, while looking at Françoise. "I've had this machine ever since I've known you, but I could not tell you. I hope from what I'll show you, you can understand why."

Françoise listened, but was on guard. Somehow she felt something was not as it was supposed to be.

"OK," is all she said.

"How about I take you to Paris, in the not too distant past? Somewhere in the twentieth century? How about ehm, 1978?"

"Seventy-seven. Seven is my lucky number."

"1977 it is, ma'am."

"When? Now?"

"Now is good. Blue jeans are good. We'll be fine."

With great skill Eddie manoeuvred the bubble into 1977's Paris. First they saw a vague image through the skin of the bubble, and when Eddie decided it was good, the bubble lowered and put them safely on the ground. Paris, 1977. They didn't know exactly where they were, but it was close to the *Champs-Élysées*. They were in a busy neighbour-hood and tried to see points of reference. After walking around, watching around, for some ten minutes a man approached them. They already noticed him following them. Close by a small group of mostly older men were watching them, they all seemed to belong together. They looked Middle Eastern, maybe Arabic?

In poor French he asked Eddie if he wanted to sell the beautiful girl, as he was referring to Françoise. She's clearly not your girlfriend, he said. Eddie was somewhat overwhelmed, but quickly responded as to make sure this awkward situation stayed under control.

"*Elle est mon sœur*," he said, thinking that would do it to get rid of the men.

"*Ç'est egal,*" the man replied, indicating he wanted to buy Françoise no matter what.

"Follow me, quickly," Eddie said to Françoise. They ran away, but were followed by the men. After one or two minutes though, the old guys gave up. Eddie directed Françoise to a dark alley, where he took out his Transformer.

"Let's go to a slightly different neighbourhood," he said with a smile.

"You know, you can't talk about this with anybody,

right? Isn't Versailles what you were studying?"

"Yes," Françoise said with a smile.

They moved towards Versailles, but they also moved in time, without realising it. It was one year later when they felt a shock that disturbed the bubble while they were landing.

"What was that?" Françoise asked.

"I don't know," Eddie replied, "I've never had something like that before."

He then noticed they had also moved in time, and adjusted the Transformer for a day earlier, as to avoid further disturbing shocks. It now was the 25th of June 1978, a day full of tourists. Nevertheless Eddie wondered how time was changed a year. In the evening they decided to book a hotel, after all, time here was only a fraction of time there.

"A room please," Eddie said.

"And one for me," Françoise said.

Eddie looked at her, somewhat surprised, separate rooms.

The next day Eddie heard in the news about a bombing in Versailles, and he realised that if he would have continued the landing in the 26th of June, they would have landed through, or maybe even in the explosion.

"Please remember Françoise, I can not stress this

enough, this is our secret, our little, big secret," he said.

233

Thirty-one

Eddie makes an appointment with Françoise. In about an hour they will have a meeting. Somehow it just fits his agenda, Eddie says.

"You know, your parallel existence is speeding up? It's almost like it's catching up with us. As a baby, you were then selected, prepared, to become a superhuman. With many others. And as you may expect, not just by accident. I think you should understand that you are more part of Operation K. then you might want to be aware of."

"That's why you wanted to see me? You think I just was sitting here watching life go by? I know Eddie, I already know. And I also know more about you then you may think I know. Whether or not I understand it all, that's a different matter. OK?"

"OK, sure, OK is KO, right?"

"Maybe not so much," Françoise then says. "What does it do for Mai, surely she is now at a point in her life where professor Kodaira expected her to be by now?"

"Professor Kodaira, professor Kodaira. Yes, I feel sorry for him, and his daughter. I tried to keep him alive, but it didn't happen. I'm sure it would have helped Mai if he was still alive. He could have explained so much more to her. You know, I can explain only so much to her, the rest she'll need to find out herself. But I, just like you, will always be there for her, right?"

"Of course, without a doubt, come on, I'm her mother. Mai is still growing up, becoming who she can be."

"And she can become anything, whatever she wants to be."

"As long as she can stay my human daughter. My lovely daughter," Françoise says, while she gently lays a hand on her own belly, as if she remembers the life that grew in her, to become Marie-Isobelle.

"How come you still look so young?" Françoise suddenly asks.

Eddie answers as if he'd been expecting that question for a long time. "OK, that answer is quite straightforward, you know. As I'm anchored in a different time frame, that time frame has a different pace, much faster than this one. Much, much faster. If you would, or could, speed up this time frame, people would see so much more, and they'd be aware of so much more. Well, yeah, we're working on it," he says with a gentle smile.

Françoise gently strokes her belly again.

"He who knows the beginnings of all things, free is his light from the realm of night."

Françoise looks at Eddie.

"What did you just say?"

"I just had to think of that quote. It's from Thoth, from a large text about wisdom, power, knowledge."

"Ah, Thoth, yes. You mean, what's it got to do with Mai?"

"I'm not yet sure how it will manifest itself, but I do see the changes. Somehow, small, but happening."

Françoise quickly looks up Thoth, to see more of what Eddie is referring to.

"The forms that ye create by brightening thy vision are truly effects that follow thy cause," she reads out loud.

"Fascinating, right?" Eddie says. "It's been my inspiration since, well forever."

Françoise looks at Eddie with a somewhat surprised look.

"Oh well, I finally get to see the real Eddie!"

"Who knows," Eddie says with a smile.

"Thoth speaks of magic, of hidden magic. Have you ever thought of how an apple transforms into thought?"

He pauses for a moment.

"I understand how matter forms into energy, but thought, that's still like magic, isn't it? Like, it's triggered in these dimensions, and yet exists in another one, and commands our behaviour in these lower dimensions. Magic, or is it?"

"We have work to do, Eddie."

"Yeah," Eddie sighs and stands up to walk to the door.

"Oh, I didn't mean..."

"No, it's alright, we have things to do. See you later."

Françoise starts reading Thoth's "The Key of Wisdom" from the beginning and finds some kind of comfort in it. She feels connected, confirmed. She smiles, it feels like meditating, she feels the magic.

"The soul in itself is cold," she thinks, "it is the heart that gives it its warmth." Above her office a hovering light orb is gently pulsating, but nobody is looking up.

Marie-Isobelle is learning to control mood-change with colour-change. Effectively she notices how she can shift the focus inward, and by doing that actually potentiates the force. Instead of just radiating it outward, it becomes stronger when she focuses it inward first. She can focus it outward by itself, but focusing it inward first makes it stronger. Fascinating. She plays with it, on her own.

"Mood changers," she thinks, "what are mood changers?"

My headaches are back.

"Growing pains," Françoise says.

"They somehow make me feel depressed," I say.

"Yup, definitely growing pains," Françoise says, while she gives me a hug.

"Let me feel."

She slowly slides her hand towards my groin.

"Oh yes, let the doctor take care of that."

She takes my hand, leads us to the bedroom and closes the door.

After about half an hour the door opens and I walk towards the kitchen to make us a cup of tea. The growing pains are gone. I take the tea out on the deck and we both sit down while Françoise puts her hand on mine.

"I love you," she says.

"I love you too," I reply.

"Shall we do it again?" she then says.

"Oh, let me at least finish my tea first," I reply with a smile, but we stay seated. I'm not sure if she meant it seriously. The tranquility is wonderful though, she is beautiful too. I take another sip of my tea.

"Did you just put lipstick on?" I ask Françoise.

She looks puzzled.

"What do you mean?"

"It looks good, tempting, seductive alright."

"No, I didn't put lipstick on, don't be silly now."

She walks inside to look into a mirror.

"OK. It was only a matter of time," she says.

"What happened?' I ask her.

"Well, you were just there, weren't you? I guess it was the last straw, I mean, not you. You know the expression!"

She starts laughing, and I laugh with her.

"Well, yes," she continues, "I guess it was supposed to happen some day. The accumulation of factors, and then the sex, may have triggered the last, ehm, straw."

I look at her and she really is radiating with life. It's like falling in love again. Fuck that tea.

Thirty-two

Agnes was sitting, waiting for Eddie to show up at their lunch meeting. Soon after he arrived they ordered their meal, and Agnes started talking about something Eddie didn't expect.

"You knew that old guy who stole the car, didn't you? I mean, did you organise it?"

Eddie looked at her, somewhat surprised.

"Wow, I actually thought you knew, didn't you?"

They went back and forth on how Agnes actually could have known, and how she just didn't.

"In a way," Agnes concluded, "in a way I thought I knew you. I didn't expect you to be that kind of... wicked."

She said it with a smile, which left Eddie disarmed.

"Well, that's kind of who I am, not?"

"Well I thought, I hoped, you would have been more straightforward with me, but it's OK, let's enjoy our lunch."

"I need to make this up to you," he said, "lunch is on me."

"It's a start," Agnes said with a friendly smile. "I'm not sure what to think of it," she continued. "Is it the right thing to do? Is it acceptable to meddle with these people's lives in the way you do?"

Eddie again looked surprised at her.

"I don't understand Agnes, this isn't new, or is it? We've been doing this for such a long time already, and now it is of concern to you? You know, we're the good guys, right?"

"I'm not sure anymore, Eddie."

Eddie looked thoughtful, serious, but then put his friendly face on again.

"You know we all love you, right?"

He paused for a moment.

"Oops, that didn't come out as supposed. I know, we know, you're a clever, caring, charming lady. And that you care about the world, your world, our world, the future world. Maybe we should remind ourselves about the cause, we're trying to create a natural force against people who want to destroy this world for religious reasons. And actually, I think it is working. Yes, I agree with you that we're using people, but we're also looking after them, right? We need those ultra-colour-sensitive people to direct, to manipulate, to save humanity's future, and they do still have their own individual lives, right?"

Agnes looked at him and gently nodded.

"I guess you're right, I may have forgotten the focus, the

blessings of getting older? But then again, you also get to see things differently."

"You know I've been able to transform into a light orb, a Sentinel, for a while? I thought it was permanent, but recently I lost it. It was fascinating though, while it lasted."

"Oh, that is fascinating! How did that happen?"

"I'm not sure. I'm not sure how I could do it, and I'm not sure about how I lost it. But, I know now the dark agent has a name. His name is Ben, he said."

"Wow, now that is first class information," she said with a slightly sarcastic tone.

"You is on a roll ma'am?" Eddie then replied.

"Oh, I'm sorry Eddie, I hear this, I hear that, and it doesn't fit in a structure."

"Now, there's my girl again, trying to make sense of it all. The thing is, I think, that it's so much more simple than what we've been looking for, that we may have missed it. I mean, for I don't know exactly how long, probably centuries, there's a group of religious people who want nothing more than provoke the second coming of their saviour. The ones that I just mentioned, who want to destroy this world to force their saviour to come back. For them. It beats me how they do not see the selfishness, the cold-heartedness of it, which is exactly the opposite of the presumed teachings of the Son of God that they believe in."

"Ah, now I see where you're getting at. And they avoid being directly involved with the, ehm, destructive actions, but instead get others to do it for them."

"All motivated by selfish greed, hunger for power, etcetera. You got it. Do you agree how simplistic it actually is? But they don't care, they don't care at all."

"The simplicity then probably fits with its brutality, right?"

"Oh dear," Eddie said, "look there, speaking of the devil, at the last table, a man and a woman, that's Ben."

Close to Ben, two tables further, there was another couple, they all belonged to Ben's team. It took a while before Eddie and Agnes saw them for who they are, their typical low-key behaviour though made them stand out. Eddie waited till he caught Ben's eye, and waved at him. At first Ben was somewhat surprised, but acted cool, and finally lightly raised his hand. Eddie was amused, and so was Agnes.

"Winning," he said.

He decided to play with them, raised up from his chair and pretended as if he was ready to leave. Ben's partner also stood up, but Eddie sat down again. The agent was confused and tried to act as if she needed to stand up for something, and sat down again. Eddie thought of doing the same act again, but he didn't. Instead he called a taxi. A minute later they left, leaving Ben's team behind.

"Winning!" Eddie said out loud in the taxi, with Agnes laughing with him.

In her apartment in Brussels, Françoise was writing her thesis, reading up on Versailles, and daydreamed about our first meeting. She knew she had been there centuries before I was. She knew that love isn't measured in time, nor in dimensions. She also knew though, that she was not who she thought she was. Somehow Versailles turned out to be way more than just a building, way more than a sun king, way more than the people who built it, way more than the sum of its parts. Way more. Somehow she had also fallen in love with a building. She laughed at the thought, it brought her in a better mood again. She decided to write another letter, but after she had written one and a half pages, she stopped. Her mind stopped. There was something else occupying her mind. It was bugging her. So much so that she decided to leave for Amsterdam that evening.

It was dark and gloomy when Françoise arrived in Amsterdam. As usual it was busy around the Amsterdam Central Station. "*It's amusing to still see so many people on bicycles*," she thought. Françoise decided to also get one from the depot in front of the train station. With her ID card the computer matched the optimal bicycle for Françoise, and within a minute her bike was presented from the underground bicycle hangar. Only drawback, Françoise thought, was that there were no humans involved in the process, well, at least not above ground, maybe underground, but then again, those would most probably be robots, either biological or mechanical. The biological robots were a dying breed though, humanity finally came to its senses. With a small backpack she cycled along Damrak, she enjoyed the wind in her face, even though it was a bit cold. At about 9:00PM she left the bike at the Lijnbaansgracht Depot, and walked the last hundred meters along the canal.

She walked up the stairs into her apartment, dropped the backpack and made herself a hot chocolate in the kitchen. Elle was not there yet, so she relaxed, warming her hands on the warm mug. She looked around in her roomy apartment, quite different from the one in Brussels. But then again, this was where she actually lived, she thought. She looked at the Mars painting, and just when she was about to stand up and walk towards it, the door opened and Elle walked in, with the baby in her arm.

"Hey Francy," she said.

"Hi Elle."

Elle walked up to Françoise and gave her a hug, baby Maribelle was sleeping.

"I'll bring her to bed, one moment please."

After a few minutes Elle returned to the room and sat down with Françoise.

"I thought you might also want one," Françoise said, pointing at the mug with hot chocolate for Elle.

"Hm, lovely, thank you! So what brings you back so soon? I thought you were staying in Brussels?"

"Well, you actually," while she looked straight at Elle. "You know, it's been bugging me for quite a while now, and I think it's way overdue to tell you."

Francoise paused for a moment.

"Tell me what?"

"You know, it's a year ago now, I brought a friend to my birthday party, and you have sex with him and have a baby."

"Is that why we're not having a birthday party this year?"

"Yes! You finally got it!"

Elle sat back, stunned, totally surprised at Françoise's outburst.

"But you know, I love you! You're my dearest. Françoise, I love you. I would never want to hurt you. I'm so sorry, I'm so sorry. I'm so sorry!"

"Then why did you do it, for God's sake!"

"I don't know, the party, him, the wine?"

"Eddie?" Françoise said.

"How, Eddie?"

"Did Eddie do something to encourage you to go down to the bedroom?"

"Oh, I don't remember. Oh wait, the wine. Eddie did suggest to go downstairs. Eddie?"

"Wine and Eddie. But that doesn't leave you off the hook, does it? Oh, I'm so mad at you!"

"Please keep it down, Maribelle is sleeping."

"Argh, why, why, why?"

"I loved him too, you know."

"Oh, for God's sake. As if there are not enough women loving him."

"I don't think it's the same as it is for you Fran. You still love him, don't you?"

"Yes!"

The next moments it was silent in the room. Elle and Françoise looked each other in the eyes, and away, and back again. Françoise started to cry, and Elle quickly put her arms around her.

"Why did he have to marry her? Oh, those stupid traditions!" Françoise said.

"It happened," Elle replied, "it just happened. Just like how you both met, in Paris."

"Oh no, we didn't just meet in Paris. Eddie arranged it. I'm sure Eddie arranged it. He arranged it without me knowing it. He suggested Versailles to me, and he arranged for me to have the apartment in Paris for free. He, even asked me to have a look at those military busts..."

It's as if all pieces of the puzzle were falling in their place for Françoise.

"He even just took me there!"

"Where?"

"Versailles."

"What do you mean Versailles, you were in Brussels?"

Françoise realised she shouldn't have said that.

"Yeah, never mind," she said.

She quickly tried to distract from the issue.

"Versailles was his thing, I don't know. Maybe he thinks he's the Sun King himself?"

Elle started to laugh.

"Yes, that would fit him right!"

Françoise realised though that Eddie actually did take her to Versailles, as a gesture for her, she thought. It confused her. Somehow she and Elle were not sharing their thoughts, consciousness, awareness anymore. It was as if there was a foggy wall between them. They both were feeling it, but didn't mention it. Somehow, slowly they seemed to be growing apart.

"I'm going to bed early," Elle said.

Françoise stayed in the living room. A bit sad, but also relieved she had finally got the issue out.

"Surreptitious, insidious," she was thinking of words describing Elle. It wasn't over yet.

Thirty-three

"Mood-changers," Eddie tells Marie-Isobelle.

"So that's what they do," Marie-Isobelle replies.

"So that's what you would do."

"And that would be enough? I mean, would I do that on my own? I guess not?"

"The point is to learn to focus, without visibly changing the colours. Otherwise they'd easily find out, right?"

"And how would I do that?"

"Well, that's what I'm here for," Eddie replies. "Imagine you're in a room full of decisionmakers, political, business, it doesn't matter. You don't want them to find out what you're doing, right? But, then again, we could even arrange for you to become one of the leaders, right? If you'd like that," Eddie says with a smile. "But you'll always have to realise that it could actually be dangerous for you if they would notice! But that's why we're here, to make sure you can control it in any way you like. OK?"

Marie-Isobelle listens to the birds, with their happy tunes. She feels excited, as if she's part of something important.

"OK!" she says.

"OK! Now what?" Eddie says enthusiastically.

"We could start with mood-change without colour change?" Marie-Isobelle suggests.

"I was thinking the same."

"Would I classify as a MODU?" she then asks.

"Why?"

"Well, would all MODUs be able to do what I can do?"

"Many, yes, but not all, yet."

"I recently was just walking down the street, and a man came walking towards me, and it was as if we were reading each other's minds, yeah, as if it was reading. He didn't blink, or whatever, he acted as if it was normal."

"Sounds like one of the older ones," Eddie replies, "not actually old, but one of the further advanced, experienced ones, I guess."

"And how do I classify?" she asks again.

"Oh, as a MODU alright, if that is what you want to hear?"

"Yeah, something like that. Like my mother."

"Of course, it's hereditary. You know that, right?"

"Yeah, my mother said so, I think."

For the next hour or so, they talk about mood-changers

and mood-change as such. But then there is an issue while, starting a mood-change session, Marie-Isobelle has trouble even starting in colour.

"No worries," Eddie says, "starting up a new procedure isn't always easy."

"It's not that, I can't seem to get the focus into myself, it's not working."

"Relax, take some tea, and you'll be alright."

After a few more minutes, and a few more attempts, it looks as if Marie-Isobelle is right, it's not working.

"Not a problem," Eddie says, trying to calm Marie-Isobelle down, "shall we try again tomorrow?"

"Yeah, sure," Marie-Isobelle replies. She is somewhat confused, but still confident. "But wait, tomorrow I'm with my parents."

"No worries, we'll get back to it when you get back."

Françoise and I are in Strasbourg again. Today will be the last special evening for club members only, to see Leonardo da Vinci's *Salvator Mundi*. We're having a ball. How many people are there? Forty? Fifty? While it seems like much, it's nothing compared to the usual crowds filling the room.

I look at his face, his eyes, how they miss the sparkling clarity of the orb, as if the restoration wasn't quite finished yet. I do not see why Leonardo would have left it like that. I watch his hand, the way it seems to bless the viewer, or the world, and copy it with my own hand, to see whether the folds would be natural or not. They look pretty natural to me. Françoise watches me and smiles.

"Are you going to bless us too?"

I feel caught out.

"Sure, fascinating, isn't it? There is so much detail on that dress, but it is missing on his hands, but then again, especially his face."

"Right, I see," Françoise responds.

"His head isn't symmetrical, see how the right side is higher, somewhat larger?"

"Could just be his hair?"

Then after a little while Françoise asks, "What do you think those three white dots are, just highlights?"

"There have been numerous dissertations on the painting already, in which the orb has had so many interpretations. I'm glad they finally caught up on the dimensional light orb interpretation. Life is more."

There may be some eight, nine people left, when the

director comes in and suggests we can have a closer look. I'm thrilled. Close by the amount of detail on the dress is even more impressive, as are the contrasts. I watch the air bubbles in the orb, as if it is filled with water. Oh, and those three highlights.

"Those highlights just look like reflections to me," I say, but while I'm saying it, I realise they could be something more. The jewellry on the dress has it too. The orb doesn't reflect any other lighted surfaces, just those three dots and some light passing through, on the dress. The dots seem to be reflections from a rather low position. "But on second thought, I'm not sure," I add.

"The eyes don't have the highlights of the orb," Françoise says, "the right eye has a dull highlight in the middle of the pupil, and the left eye has a highlight on the right of it."

I look up a picture of the *Mona Lisa*, and notice similar facial properties, especially the size and the shape of the nose stands out. But quickly I put it away again.

"You can overanalyse," Françoise says with a smile.

"You're right," I say.

We take a little more distance, and after some five minutes we say goodbye to the *Salvator*. On our way home the scenery seems more artistic than usual. The Sentinel doesn't mind.

Marie-Isobelle is on her way to us, and takes a taxi for the last part. We could have waited, but there are only two seats in my car.

When we get home I decide to look up the *Salvator Mundi* again, it may be some ten, fifteen minutes till Marie-Isobelle is here, and I'm actually more intrigued by the painting than I was before.

Wenceclaus Hollar's etching, from 1650, should be an accurate reproduction of da Vinci's *Salvator Mundi*. The painting shows a Christ figure looking at the observer, the etching shows a Christ figure looking just past the observer, similarly to the *Mona Lisa*, but there the *Mona Lisa* looks just past to the other side of the observer. Also, the painting shows less of a beard, and has some resemblance to the *Mona Lisa* figure, even though the Christ figure is still very vague, too vague. Historically one of the most expensive paintings, and also still one of the most disputed ones. A strange combination, still.

I hear Marie-Isobelle coming in, and I'm still somewhat pulled out of the here and now by the painting. Marie-Isobelle doesn't notice when she enters the room. I didn't notice that her lips had changed, but then again, the lighting wasn't favourable for such an observation.

"Hi mum, hi dad, I'm back!"

I walk towards her and give her a hug, as does Françoise.

"Hm, that feels awkward," Marie-Isobelle says.

"Yeah, I was feeling the same," Françoise responds.

I look at them both to see what is going on.

"It doesn't feel like the last time, it doesn't feel normal, funny, mum?"

"I don't know darling, come give me another hug."

Marie-Isobelle hugs her mother one more time.

"It still feels weird, mum."

"Yeah, let it rest for now, I'll get you a cup of tea, right?"

"Right, mum."

"How was the trip?" I ask her.

"Good, nothing unusual."

And then I notice the colour of her lips.

"I thought your lips had changed to the colour of your tongue? Like purple?"

"Yes," she says.

"It looks like normal again, I mean, like the way they were before."

"Your dad is right," Françoise confirms.

Marie-Isobelle walks to the bathroom and watches her face, her tongue, lips, and gets closer to the mirror. Turns her head for a different lighting, and comes back to us.

"It's almost gone!" she says. "It already felt different on the way here, it felt as if I was losing a sense of dimension. So it was real."

She sits down and stares towards the window, and then looks at Françoise and me.

"Am I losing it?" she asks.

"No, you're not losing it!" Françoise says laughing.

"It looks like it, though!" Marie-Isobelle responds. "Argh, I don't like this."

I reach out my hand towards her and she grabs it, squeezes it, and gives me a kiss on my hand.

"Don't worry," I say, "you'll be alright."

I was right. After Marie-Isobelle has been with us for some four, five days, her colours have come back, and also the way she could see, sense her deeper reality, her colourful dimensional reality. Happy days are here again. She's sitting on the lawn, against a tree, doing some reading I guess. She looks happy indeed, I'm happy. She notices that I'm watching her, and throws me a kiss. I throw one back, while

I'm thinking about Marie-Isobelle's condition. She came back to us from Amsterdam and seemed to be losing her colours, maybe even lost it, and now that she is with us she seems to be normal again, her normal that is.

"Did you see that?" Marie-Isobelle calls out gently.

I look up and see a small orange orb-like bubble slowly fly towards me.

"Mwah!" she says, while the little ball splashes on my cheek. "I love you!"

"I love you too, Mai!"

Happy days are here again, I feel.

The Sentinel is content.

Eddie is in contemporary Versailles. In the library he made himself comfortable with some old books and a coffee. He enjoys the experience. A girl from the library walks up to him.

"Please sir, could you please not put your shoes on the table?"

Eddie quickly sits upright.

"Oops, sorry, I guess I got carried away. Won't happen again."

"Thank you sir."

Eddie checks the bag under his legs, and then places it forward, so he can put his feet up again. He looks a bit smug alright. The black coffee is great. He sighs and smiles while amusedly he looks around. Next time he should bring a cigar, he thinks. "Nah, it's good."

Thirty-four

It still lies there, the stone: a year ago
I placed it there myself; I call to mind
the place quite well, right next to that skewed pine
and the white sand-path to the heath below.

I mused: 'I do as pharaohs did before;
the dread's the same that asked of me and them:
all perishes: am I not who I am,
and was and shall remain for evermore?' –

I'd lain down, with my head close by the stone;
which, in the gathering dark, seemed to have grown
a monument, Egyptian – old and great.

A small star high above. I thought: 'It gave
its light when they were building Ramses' grave.'
And I felt clearly: we were of one date.

Françoise was reading from the little booklet, "Full of God and tiny pancakes". She thought it was funny and serious at the same time, and a great way to provoke the mind. She put it aside when she heard Maribelle waking up. Elle would be away for just a few minutes.

"Look what I found," she said, entering the room, "at the gallery around the corner."

With the baby on her arm, Françoise looked at a small ceramic teapot, light beige with a soft pink lid on it. Françoise came closer, and then suddenly moved up, looking at Elle.

"Is that...," she asked.

"Yes," Elle answered, "it's actually called, *Vagina teapot.*"

For a second it was silent, then they burst out laughing, but quickly controlled it, as not to frighten baby Maribelle.

"It's beautiful!" Françoise said.

"Right, isn't it?"

"It's so funny! Let's clean it up and have some tea!"

And so, a few minutes later Maribelle got to drink from Elle, and Elle and Françoise drank tea from the *Vagina teapot.*

"Is it old or new?" Françoise asked.

"Early twenty-first century, the girl said. But she didn't exactly know. She'd ask the shop owner when she was back, she said."

With summer almost around the corner, Françoise and Elle seemed to have become closer again, even though they did not share their consciousness anymore. Maybe growing up meant growing more apart, at least for them. Or was it more like letting go, like freedom? They weren't sure.

I wasn't sure what to think anymore. I had noticed myself contemplating more often. Was the world changing for the good, or was it changing for the bad, again? It was as if they were mood swings, but then again, I wasn't that kind of guy, I thought. I was looking forward to the summer, taking our baby out on the beach, playing with the sand, or to the forest, cool, and full of life. With Mai sleeping in my arms it was easy to forget time.

After about an hour she woke up, Joan was already waiting. I took a picture of them both, Joan the happy mother, and Mai the still somewhat sleepy, wondering what this was about, daughter. It was then that I felt different, a connection that I wasn't aware of before. Mai looked at me as if she could look straight into my mind. I loved her, with all of my heart, and she knew it. She then smiled.

It felt as if time was changing, was it because of how intense the experience of being a father was? I wasn't sure. On the one hand it felt as if I was seeing and understanding so much more, as if I was seeing the sense of it all, and on the other hand it felt as if it was the exact opposite, or as if I could see from different perspectives, seeing the sense and nonsense of it all. Was it all nonsense? What have we achieved? We got rid of the ever-increasing control from the AI community, we got rid of the corrupting financial control system, we got rid of the corrupting elites. But what did we get in return? More freedom? More happiness? More truth? I often worried about the future for Mai as life wasn't as I expected it to be, was it really better? But then I looked around me, and realised life is good. With Joan and Mai sitting comfortably together on the couch I decided to take a ride, as the weather seemed so great.

I asked Joan if it was OK if I went for a little ride, and she was alright with it. I checked the hydrogen and the tyres, and off I was. It felt funny, driving on my own. Little meandering country roads, along small streams, through little patches of forest. Why did it all seem so gentle and small?

After some thirty minutes a noticed a sign for the *Autobahn*. Yup, that's what I was going to do. Five minutes later I found myself driving quite a bit beyond the 200 km/h mark, 237, 242, when a slow vehicle suddenly changed lanes. It was the moment when I realised I was not just me, not just a husband, but above all, a father.

When I looked for a moment out of the side window I saw a Sentinel was hovering with me. I had never seen one during daylight before, but I quickly realised what it was. I raised my index finger at it, as if greeting, as if saying "thank you". I saw a small flash, and then it was gone. From that moment on I decided to just enjoy the ride, without the thrill of speed. Well, almost.

In Amsterdam it seemed as if the dark agents were busy with something else, as they were hardly ever close to Elle and Françoise anymore. It was as if they had different priorities now. Just for now? It was a happy time though; while Françoise was spending more time on her thesis, either in Brussels or in Amsterdam, Eddie came around more often, like a caring friend. They often talked about issues like awareness, focal points and focal concentration. Clearly Agnes had made him clear of something. Sometimes getting older has its advantages.

The canals in Amsterdam seemed clearer than ever before, but Elle realised their danger as little Maribelle did her first steps outside the house. She acted as if she had an extra sense of hearing car tyres, or anything speeding up. She also looked up more often, to see if there was a Sentinel near, and meanwhile trying to give her baby all the attention that she needed. Multitasking wasn't really her thing, she concluded, while she actually was quite good at it. They heard music that sounded like a Latin rhythm and Elle took Maribelle by the hands, doing a sweet tiny dance together. Elle noticed some people watching and smiled at them. A little further away Elle thought she recognised one of Ben's dark agents, one of the women. She waved, Elle waved back and took Maribelle on her arm. The agent walked on and Elle sat down on a step. She sighed and looked at Maribelle, who was looking back at Elle with a glorious smile. The agent turned her head once more, looked at Elle and Maribelle, smiled, and walked on again.

On her way back up to the apartment Elle opened the mailbox and took out a few letters, the address on the top one started with "*de ouders/verzorgers van Marie-Isobelle*", she quickly read it and put it with the other letters. It was just another official letter from the health department, those nosy bureaucrats, she thought.

When I came back home I let the car cool down outside and swiftly checked inside if everything was OK with Mai and Joan. Of course it was. I walked back outside to sit on the little wall. I heard the car cooling down and watched its sculptural beauty. If ever I would marry a car, this one would be it! The thought amused me so much I almost started laughing out loud. Joan saw me and later asked what that was. She looked at me with a smile and a little frown, and then simply said: "OK." Joan wasn't of the worrying kind, at least she hardly ever showed it. She was more of the caring kind, even though that would sometimes bring worries, oh well.

"You could always apply for AI status!" she then said, "I think that's still possible! That would make it possible for you?"

I was glad she said it in a way that was amusing, not threatening. Somehow my sense of guilt was playing up again.

"Yes dear," I said, "I'll think about it."

Somehow I almost felt sorry for the car, that she didn't have a real voice in it. Hm, she? I already felt sorry for her when we had that issue with the polluted hydrogen, it was labelled as a terrorist attack, but I'd qualify it as a terrorist action at best, just a polluting action probably. I felt a slight headache coming on, but it didn't became one really. I realised that my headaches weren't as frequent as they used to be, while I did feel different, a different kind of consciousness, a different kind of awareness. I felt it on the *Autobahn,* it was as if I could feel the other drivers considering to change lanes, before the car actually started doing it. I could feel Joan, I could feel Mai watching me even though I knew she could not see me.

Françoise wrote me a letter again, this time she did send it, asking if she could see me, or if I would come to see her. There was something in her letters that I could not quite understand. Was she manipulating me? Was she just expressing her love? Mostly it felt so overwhelming, so caring, so warm, that it always triggered a response from me that would somehow make it worse, or better, depending on which perspective one would choose. She asked me to choose, while not thinking about her at all, not thinking about Joan, just to think about me, myself. I wasn't that kind of a person, and I thought she would know. It was that kind of questions, suggestions, that made me feel on edge, because after all, I did love her, and I thought, she did love me. And everything she said in that letter was so warm, even hot, sexy, caring, about love, our love, whatever that would be.

Thirty-five

"Oh man, it's hot today," I say to myself.

"Oh dad, it's so hot today," Marie-Isobelle says, a little later calling from Amsterdam. "It's the fourth day in a row. People are sweating like pigs, hm, I don't know if I've ever seen pigs sweating, but anyhow!"

"Yeah, well, it's hot alright, I just saw your mother walking naked in the garden, so, well, you know."

"Oh dad, please stop it, or I'll tell mum!"

"Sorry, won't do it again. Beside the heat, is everything OK Mai?"

"Yes, sure. Apart from that yesterday I actually felt as if I was losing my mood colours again, you know, feeling and projecting. Just when Eddie has been helping me to improve it."

"Hm, are you still drinking enough with this hot weather?" I ask her.

"Of course," she says, "even during the evening, extra tea."

"Hm, if it continues, you could ask Eddie if he knows?"

"If he knows what?"

"If he knows if there's something going on, something to consider? I'll ask your mother in a minute, OK?"

"OK, catch you later!"

In the shade of a large parasol Eddie is reading a text from the Emerald Tablets of Thoth, and wonders if it relates to the dark agents. After reading it, he leaves the page open and ponders over it.

Turn thy thoughts inward not outward. Find thou the Light-Soul within. Know that thou are the Master. All else is brought from within. Grow thou to realms of brightness. Hold thou thy thought on the Light. Know thou are one with the Cosmos, a flame and a Child of the Light.
Now to thee give I warning: Let not thy thought turn away. Know that the brightness flows through thy body for aye. Turn not to the Dark-Brightness that comes from the Brothers of Black. But keep thine eyes ever lifted, thy soul in tune with the Light. Take ye this wisdom and heed it. List to my Voice and obey. Follow the pathway to brightness, and thou shalt be One with the way.

The phone rings and Eddie answers it.

"*Bonjour mademoiselle,*" he says eloquently.

"*Bonjour monsieur,*" she replies in style. "Eddie," she continues, "do you have time to talk?"

"Sure, go ahead, oh wait, are you at home?"

"Yes, why?"

"If you go out your front door, to the right, and turn left over the bridge, then you'll see me sitting under a large yellow and white parasol, enjoying life and a cool beer. See you in a minute?"

"Sure," Marie-Isobelle says laughing.

After a minute or two Marie-Isobelle approaches the large yellow and white parasol.

"*Bonjour* your highness the sun king," she says, referring to the yellow, golden colour under the parasol.

"Yes, it's the good life, isn't it? Please take a seat."

While she sits down she notices the text Eddie was reading.

"I'm not disturbing you with anything?" she asks.

"No, no, of course not, not you!"

"OK then. You know, the inward focus we talked about, to make the beam more powerful, it doesn't work anymore."

Eddie looks at her and seems surprised.

A waitress comes to the table and asks Marie-Isobelle if she wants something to drink.

"A mango juice please."

"Ah, you don't drink alcohol, right?"

"Right."

"So, what's the matter, baby?"

Marie-Isobelle notices the slightly unusual tone, and realises this might not be his first beer this afternoon. She decides to discuss the issue anyway.

"OK, are you listening? I just said the inward focus doesn't seem to work anymore."

"Oh, sure, well, actually I don't know. It's so damn hot today, don't you think?"

He gazes at two young women walking by in colourful, short flowery dresses.

"I didn't know they still make those flower dresses, did you?"

"Oh, you're useless today," while she takes a sip from her juice. She decides to drop her issue for now. "What were you reading?"

"As a matter of fact I think it would surprise you, I think."

"Well, surprise me then."

"You know Thoth?"

"Todd who?"

"No Thoth, T-H-O-T-H, Thoth."

"Oh, Thoth."

"Yes, Thoth."

"Ehm, no, not really, a little bit, maybe."

After talking about Thoth for almost an hour Eddie's mind seems to clear up.

"There is another way to find your inner focus," he then explains, "through your ears. Shower water over your ears. It's actually a similar noise as when with the Transformer when you go into the moving mode, after which it is silent again. Maybe you remember?"

The next morning Marie-Isobelle takes a shower, she's slightly tilting her head backward and lets the water flow over her ears.

"Ah, that's the sound," she thinks.

She moves a little bit with her head, changing the sounds, and slowly moves her focus inward, with the sounds. It fascinates her, and gently keeps moving her head. Then she finds a position where both her ears seem fully emerged under the streaming water. It's a full sound, where nothing else gets through. Fully immersed under streaming water, like in a waterfall. A warm waterfall. Comfortable, a separate world. She tries to stay stable in one position, sometimes shielding her nose as to breath more easily. And then she finds a position where she can stand without moving, just breathing, listening to the streaming water, inside her head. Ten seconds, thirty seconds, a minute, two minutes. And then, she feels something changing, a red colour pops from her head, softly, and another one more clearly, green, orange, softly popping away.

"Yes," she says softly. "Yes!"

Then more colours come at the same time, and then... it stops. One more, and it stops again. Completely.

"I could feel it!" she says out loud.

She could feel it again, and then it was gone. She stays under the shower for a little longer, and then slightly confused she picks up her towel and starts drying herself. It was like an old-fashioned engine, starting up, sputtering, seemingly getting there, and then not. There's a Sentinel watching her from above, sensing, more than watching, or is it?

She calls Eddie, but he doesn't answer and then decides to go outside. It's a beautiful morning. On her way downstairs she hears two other people, who also seem to live in the apartment building, talk about the water.

"It smells of chlorine, chemicals," one of them says.

Marie-Isobelle then realises that, indeed, there was a smell to the water, but then again, every now and then that does happen. She walks outside and greets another neighbour who just leaves the building next door.

"Good morning!"

"Good morning!" Marie-Isobelle answers, "does your tap water also smell so awfully of chlorine?"

"Well, no, not that I have noticed," the neighbour answers. "How so?"

"Oh, in our building a few people noticed it. Well, never mind. Cheers, have a great day!"

"Have a great day!" the neighbour responds.

While she walks along the canals, enjoying the birds, the sun through the trees, she thinks about the shower. How pleasant it was, raising her senses, and then gone again.

Then Eddie calls.

"Morning Mai, how are you. You called?"

"Morning Eddie, yes. You know, that idea you mentioned about focusing inward through listening, the ears, I did it this morning, and it worked, sort of. It seemed to work, and then it was gone again. Well, it seemed to start to work, that's how it felt."

Eddie doesn't respond immediately, he's thinking.

"OK," he then says, "interesting, it starts, and then stops."

"It seems to start, and then stops," Marie-Isobelle clarifies.

"Yeah, yeah," Eddie says pensively. "I don't know, I don't know, I'll have to think about it. Let me call you again, OK?"

"Sure, thanks. Later!"

Marie-Isobelle continues her walk along the canals, and after some ten, fifteen minutes decides to have a tea at the tea house.

After the tea is served, she opens the lid and smells the tea.

"Hm, it smells great," she tells the waiter. She then realises the tea water doesn't have the slightest hint of nasty smells, chemicals, or whatever. She then goes on enjoying the moment. Happy people, and only a few tourists, yet.

After a little while she starts thinking about the conversation she overheard that morning and decides she might check with other neighbours about their water.

"Yup, that's something to do later," she tells herself.

On the other side a group of schoolchildren walk by, they too are enjoying themselves. A few grandparents behind them it seems, trying to keep up with the pace. Ah, they're not the last ones, there's more coming. Marie-Isobelle watches them, relaxed, enjoying her tea, and a cookie.

Marie-Isobelle decides to give her dad a call.

"Hi dad!"

"Good morning Mai! Is it still morning?"

"Sure, here it is. It's a wonderful morning. How's it with you and mum?"

"Good, your mum and I were just about to have a stroll in the city and have lunch there. How about you?"

"Is mum at home today?"

"Yeah, she didn't feel all too well this morning, so she decided to take the day off. She seems almost better now, I think," while I look at Françoise to check if I'm correct. She nods with a smile.

"Oh good, tell her I love her!"

"I love you too!" Françoise says, as she was listening to our conversation.

Marie-Isobelle realises she's on a public terrace and slightly lowers her voice.

"Oh sorry mum, mwah! You too dad, mwah!"

"Mwah! Mwah!" she hears.

"Oh mum, do you think chlorine in the drinking water could affect my senses?"

"Oh sure," Françoise replies, "that's why such chemicals are not used anymore in most places, but then again, you do still see it in some places, especially large cities, at a bare minimum though. I wouldn't think it's in the water in Amsterdam though. Why? You think it's in your water?"

"Well, yeah, that's actually what I was thinking. I was thinking of checking with the neighbours if they have the same issue, as I heard it this morning from neighbours in my building, and the neighbour next door didn't have an issue."

"I think that's a good idea, checking with the other neighbours, and see if there's something wrong with your water supply," Françoise says.

"I think your mother is right, as usual," I say.

That afternoon Marie-Isobelle checks with her neighbours, the few that are home, but still it appears there's only an issue with her apartment building, so she checks with water supply, and she checks with maintenance, to see if they would ask a plumber to have a look at the water pipes.

The next day a plumber gets under the building to check the plumbing on the water pipes. It all seems OK, but then his eye falls on a grey box on the wall that the incoming water pipes go through.

"That's a bit unusual," he thinks.

After checking with the manager they decide to have a closer look at the box and open it. It actually isn't easy to open as there are no visible screws on it.

"You can break it open, if you can fix it afterwards," the manager says.

"Sure, why not," the plumber says.

In the meantime a few more people have gathered around the mystery box in the cellar. The plumber takes a small crowbar from his toolbox, wriggles it behind the wall and the box, and the next moment water splashes from the wall and the box drops on the floor.

"Quickly, the stopcock."

Luckily it is just about a metre away, the manager closes it and the water stops.

In the water on the floor the damaged box lays open. The water pipe, however, is also damaged. They decide to have a look at the box and open it some more. They see several different vials, different colours. A strong chemical smell comes from it as fluid seeps from the vials.

"Chlorine?" Marie-Isobelle asks.

"Yup, surely that's one of them," the plumber says.

Thirty-six

Elle had registered the name of Maribelle as Marie-Isobelle and nobody else seemed to know, not even Françoise. Maribelle was a happy, healthy and very clever child. The look from her eyes was intriguing. She could capture anyone with just her eyes, stop them in their tracks and nobody seemed to realise what was going on. Maribelle just seemed to enjoy it, she'd play with it until she'd have enough of it. The M-institute was a place where they both felt at home, at least Elle did, ever since Eddie had mentioned it to her. Maribelle just loved to play with those people.

"She's a mood changer," they told Elle.

"Yes, of course she is," Elle replied with a smile.

"She's got a great future ahead of her."

"Yeah, sure," Elle replied with a smile, not really knowing what she replied to.

My mechanical watch really acted weird, sometimes it was too fast, sometimes it was too slow, though my impression as if time was speeding up seemed consistent, and I was not sure how to feel about that. Mai and Joan didn't really seem to care, it was as if they had time of their own. Even though Joan worked just a few hours per week, half of the time she took Mai with her. I thought it would be too distracting, but Joan said it was actually the opposite, inspiring. As long as they both were happy, I didn't mind. And it did give me some time for myself too, not bad.

Françoise had asked me again if I would like to come over, and this time I said yes.

I walked up the stairs to her apartment. When I was almost at the top I saw Françoise standing in the doorway, she was wearing an elegant dark dress, leaning with her left shoulder against the wall. The view nailed me to the stairs. A sweet smell. Colours started changing, from cool blue to bright blue to purple, and then yellow, soft yellow, almost orange. They were her colours. With her left hand she slowly and gently pulled her dress backwards, and with her right hand she slowly lifted it up, showing her beautiful legs. And then with her index finger, still on her slightly lifted dress, she tapped on her belly, pointing down, while looking me straight in the eyes. "Come here", she softly said with a warm smile and a voice to die for…

I was still nailed to the ground. My God, she was so incredibly beautiful, it almost felt as if I was under a spell. How did she radiate those beautiful colours, yes, they were hers. She pulled me towards her, like with an invisible beam, yet it was so colourful.

"More like a fishing net than a beam," I thought.

I took the last step up the stairs and walked towards her. Still those wonderful colours were surrounding us, filling the space, especially filling the space between us, as it became smaller and smaller. She pulled her dress up even more and let it drop, putting her arms around me. She kissed me, on my lips, warm, passionate, overwhelming. Her colours seem to be whirling around us, as if I was becoming part of them, as if they were becoming part of me, it seemed. Françoise was becoming part of me, and I started to fight it off.

Within a second Françoise let go.

"What's wrong?" she asked.

The colours were gone, the whirling emotion was gone. It was as if I was in a different world. Which world I didn't know.

"What's wrong?" she asked again.

"I don't know," I said. "I don't know, I don't know!"

In a way that I didn't know about myself, I let myself slide down against the wall. I felt defenceless, and yet I wasn't. While I sat on the floor Françoise came down, and sat down on my lap. With two hands she held my face and started kissing me again. The colours were gone, it seemed. At least I didn't see them.

"What's wrong, darling?" she asked again, and moved to sit right next to me. She grabbed my hand and squeezed it, as if to bring something out that she was hoping to see.

"I don't know, darling," I said.

Above her apartment a Sentinel was vibrating.

After some five minutes we went inside her apartment, and sat down on the couch in the living room. The room looked lovely, the light, the flowers, even that Mars painting looked different. Softer, fresher, could a painting be kind? I looked at Françoise again, and she at me. She took my hand again, but didn't squeeze it now. She just held it, gently stroking with the other hand. We looked at each other, without saying a word. I saw a tear in her eyes, and then we hugged. I felt so happy and horrible at the same time.

Thirty-seven

It has taken only two days for Marie-Isobelle to regain her normal colours. In front of her mirror she's sticking out her tongue and makes a little victory dance. She's made an appointment with Chisato and Eddie, they'll meet in about five minutes at Felix Meritis.

When Marie-Isobelle arrives, Chisato is already waiting. She listens to the music that's playing and gently dances while sitting on her chair.

"Bloom," Marie-Isobelle says.

"King of Limbs," Chisato answers.

A little hug, and Marie-Isobelle sits opposite Chisato.

"Did you already order?"

"Yeah, a pot of Quince & Ginger green tea, if that's OK with you?"

"Sure, great! Nothing of Eddie yet?"

"Not in the slightest."

"You know what happened to me?" Marie-Isobelle asks.

Chisato looks and waits for what is coming.

"I think they've tried to poison me."

Then Eddie approaches the table and gives both

Chisato and Marie-Isobelle a small hug.

"Poison?" he asks. "Nah, I don't think so. If they wanted to poison you they would have been more careful, and would have chosen a personal approach. I think they just wanted to stop you, not to kill you."

At the table next to theirs a girl turns around, as if she'd been listening to what Eddie said, but then quickly turns around again.

"How did you grow a beard so quickly?" Marie-Isobelle then asks.

"Oops, forgot to shave," Eddie then says. He pauses for a moment.

"I might as well say it now, then. I planned to tell you anyhow," while he looks at Chisato, "that's what I owe to my friend Hikari Kodaira, right?"

"Tell me what?"

"About the colours, the mood-colours your father had been working on. Your father knew you could also do it, but tried to keep it from you. Keep it from you, to protect you. I know he told you a lot, but he didn't tell you everything. But I think eventually he would have told you."

"What? That I can change moods? I already knew that."

"Your father didn't yet tell you, I think, how far-reaching

it could be, to what purpose."

Both Chisato and Marie-Isobelle are waiting for what comes next.

"One. My beard."

Then he lowers his voice and comes closer to Marie-Isobelle and Chisato. They come closer to Eddie.

"Marie-Isobelle already knows. I have a time-travelling machine, it's the Transformer. It's here in my bag."

Eddie slightly lifts up his bag.

"When I travel to the past time goes slower, which is why I can be there for a month while you'd be missing me here for a day. Hence the beard. I forgot to shave."

"Did you go to Versailles, Paris, again?" Marie-Isobelle asks.

"Guilty as charged," Eddie answers with a smile.

Chisato looks at them, but has no clue what they're talking about.

"I'll tell you later," Marie-Isobelle says to Chisato.

Eddie nods.

"You were telling about a purpose," Marie-Isobelle continues.

"The purpose," Eddie repeats.

"Wait," Chisato says, "I think I have to pee. Excuse me."

"Sure," Eddie replies, "we'll be here while you're gone."

"Sure?" Marie-Isobelle asks, while hinting at the bag.

"Sure," Eddie says again.

"OK, I could try, right?"

"About that water in your apartment," Eddie then says, "did you find out more about it?"

"Oh yes, those little bottles contained fluoride, chlorine and barium, so yeah, that's why I was thinking they were trying to poison me. You know, like Chisato's father."

"Ah, no, no, no, then they'd be poisoning the entire building. You see? They want to control you, not poison you. Well, that's what I think. But you're building a barrier around you, so it will become harder and harder for them to do that. Right?"

Eddie pours some tea for the three of them. Tea with a *speculaasje.*

"So, the purpose," Chisato says while she sits down again. "Oh, thank you for the tea."

"You're welcome," Eddie says. "The purpose. OK, you know your father and I knew each other for quite a long time, right? Your father knew I had this little machine, the Transformer, even though he wanted to have nothing to do with it. In a way I think he even hated it. I think he hated it because he realised what could come of it, and how he'd be involved. And how you could be involved."

"What does that little machine do, the Transformer?"

"OK, I'll tell you bluntly, and you'll have to believe for now that it's not nonsense, as Marie-Isobelle can confirm."

Chisato looks at Marie-Isobelle, who nods with her head.

"Like I just said, it really is a time machine," Eddie says quietly.

"You're not joking, right?!" Chisato says quietly also.

"A time machine," Eddie repeats quietly.

"And what would that have to do with us?"

"I, come, from the future. I've come to make sure some things happen to secure a better future for us all."

"Right," Chisato says as if Eddie just said something silly and simple. "Or not right," she continues.

"To secure a global society of healthy, well-educated, well-informed, and well-caring people, some significant changes need to be made. As opposed to a group, an organisation, of religious fanatics, whose only goal is to destroy the global civilisation as soon as possible. The Armageddon fanatics as we refer to them. We found, and your father found, that there are people with special mental talents, who can change things significantly. They can influence the machine of political policymakers. People like you and Marie-Isobelle, and there are already many more."

He now looks at Marie-Isobelle.

"We have talked about this for quite some time already, how to use and improve your talents, right?"

"Oh, I've seen that from Marie-Isobelle already," Chisato responds.

Eddie again looks at Marie-Isobelle. They look each other straight in the eyes.

"We've just communicated a few things with each other," Eddie tells Chisato. "See what happens."

Marie-Isobelle slightly turns her head towards another table, there are eight people sitting at it. She focuses inward for some five, ten seconds and something changes at that table. It's as if they all are standing up to go to the bathroom, at the same time.

"What did you do?" Chisato asks.

"I've made them all want to pee urgently," she says with a somewhat serious smile.

All three start to laugh, but not too loud.

"And how is that going to change the world?"

"I can make whole groups think positively, kindly, in a

constructive way, right Eddie?"

"Right, but it's a very serious issue."

He pauses for a moment, and again looks at Marie-Isobelle.

"You know, what one sees as a powerful instrument, someone else may see as a powerful weapon. And there's a serious danger in that, but then again, we're working on making you stronger in defending yourself, right?"

He pauses for a moment.

"You have a great future ahead of you. A child of the light."

"A child of the light?"

"Yup. That was from Thoth, you know, T-H-O-T-H."

They both start laughing.

"Yeah, I know."

Chisato laughs with them, but then turns to a serious face.

"You know a lot of people see that as satanic matter, don't you?" she says.

"Dark matter, you mean?" Eddie says in a somewhat obtrusive way.

"Ah, dark matter," Marie-isobelle says, "my kind of thing. Dark, dark matter. I think that what we call dark matter is just the shadow of a higher dimension, the vehicle and fluid structure in which this higher dimension moves and exists."

Eddie just sits there, speechless.

Chisato looks at Marie-Isobelle.

"Where did that come from?"

"Thoth?" Marie-Isobelle says laughing.

"Oh, you're just, you're just pulling my leg!"

"Not really," Eddie says, "come, let's get some tea before it all gets cold."

38 - 39 - 40

A few days had passed. Eddie and I had a long talk about Françoise, he told me things about her that I didn't know before. We talked about Joan, and Mai, I told him things he didn't know before. It was complicated. In a way I had the impression that Eddie had grown to be more of a friend then I expected him to be.

I told him about the headaches I used to have, which seemed to have vanished, and instead I felt as if I lived in something like a higher consciousness, a higher awareness, a different consciousness, a different awareness. Which I thought, also would be the reason why I could see those colours around Françoise.

"Those colours were real," Eddie said, "but you are also right, not everyone can see, or feel them."

"Are they a blessing, or a curse?"

"Haha, there you got me," Eddie said. "I truly couldn't say, but I lean more towards a blessing, don't you think?"

"At some point I felt as if Françoise was hailing me, like with a beam, and then it felt more as if I was caught in a net. A very unusual net though, warm, trustful, sexy."

At that point I felt as if I was telling too much, maybe too much of that which belonged to just Françoise and me, so I stopped talking. Eddie noticed.

"You're right," he said, "some things are not meant to be shared with outsiders. Sharing is caring, but not all sharing is caring," he continued with a smile.

Eddie knew the inevitable was coming, he didn't say a word, the more remarkable was his care though, his unmanly care, I thought.

While we were talking, above us, a pulsating light orb was gently glowing, it changed from an opaque light ball to a transparent light ball, a Sentinel. I could feel it, I could feel it hovering close by, it made me feel safe, even though I didn't know why, as I had never seen it performing any kind of protective actions.

"What about the Sentinels?" I asked Eddie.

"What about them?" he replied.

"I feel as if that, in a way, they are part of this, aren't they?"

"Yes, I think so. I've had the pleasure of being in their realm, if only for a short while. It's different, very different. It's being without being, seeing without seeing, consciousness, yes, awareness, not as we know it. Very, very different.

Would I prefer to always live like them? Actually, no. I think the beauty of human life on Earth lies in its limitations, its hurdles, its challenges. Challenges in ways that are only possible here, experiences that can only be experienced here, both in time and in space, and yet, there's the idiots who want to destroy it, just because they believe in a second coming, and want it as soon as possible, with the help of some greedy, selfish, cold-hearted destructive people. In a way it's even funny, if it wasn't so sad, humans for sale to do the destructive, dirty work. Destruction for selfish profit, it's been going on for way too long."

He paused to take a swig from his drink.

"They won't get it, because it's got nothing to do with love, they don't understand love, they don't understand how they don't understand love, and even more, how love is a unique experience in this life on Earth."

Eddie and I looked each other in the eyes. Vulnerable, honest, truthful and immensely powerful. I could handle it. Eddie then had an idea.

"Why don't we arrange a meeting, eye to eye, between you, Joan and Françoise? Or even with Elle? And I can be there, to be of assistance? I think we need to get it right, right?"

"I think you have a point, I'll discuss it with Joan," I said.

"Good, we could arrange a meeting, and I could even chauffeur you around with my car. We'll talk about it when I get back in a few days. OK?"

"OK."

Eddie left with his car, for some business, he said. He actually went to Stuttgart and further up north again, to visit a few of the couples he managed. Yeah, it was as if that was some kind of family management, colourful family management. He actually made that round trip on a regular basis: Amsterdam, Strasbourg, Stuttgart, Leipzig, Berlin, Hamburg, Groningen and back to Amsterdam. Not always all of them on the same trip though, he always managed some time off in between visits, for himself. The more time he spent in our time, the more he seemed to manage time for himself. He was changing. Was he adapting? Was he choosing life in our time, our dimensions? In a way he was also worried, as the more time he spent in our dimensions, our time, the more he got attached to it. And he loved to drive his old-fashioned hydrogen car around. Stuck to Earth, the wind around your head, the trees rushing by, the sounds of the trees, the simple, glorious sounds of speed.

"If only humans would realise," he thought.

Elle and Françoise responded enthusiastically after Eddie talked with them about arranging a meeting with Joan and me. Finally they thought, finally meeting the other woman. Even Françoise was enthusiastic, Eddie was a bit surprised. But then again, the idea had been lingering around for such a long time already. Release.

Joan and I already discussed it a year ago, even though in the meantime she had some doubts. But then again, she was looking forward to it, and so was I.

Marie-Isobelle and Chisato were reading and discussing the Tablets of Thoth. It was pleasant that the temperature had dropped. At least they could be outside now and move without breaking a sweat.

"What if it's all just fake?" Chisato said. "Compare it with other religious, or semi-religious scriptures. The repeating pattern, you know?"

"Yeah, I know what you mean," Marie-Isobelle said, "to me, it is inspiring, but like my father said, it's easy to take from such texts and interpret them the way it suits you, or even discard whatever doesn't suit you. Or even rewrite it for that matter, as happened numerous times, right?"

Marie-Isobelle's phone rang.

"Hi dad."

"Hi Mai, how are you?"

"Good."

"OK, your mother and I decided to come to Amsterdam, either tomorrow or the day after. Does that suit you?"

"Of course, I'll be here anyhow."

"OK, we'll see you then. Kisses! And from your mum!"

"You too, mwah, mwah, mwah!"

Chisato looked amused.

"And you too," Marie-Isobelle said, "mwah!"

Chisato laughed, and threw kisses back.

"What time is it? Let's get something to eat!"

Françoise and I had decided to pay her a visit, the weather was promising for the next few days, great for a ride. We decided to make it the day after tomorrow, when there would be less traffic on the road.

The first part was easy, on the world famous German Autobahn. It was always amusing, driving on the left lane, and if you weren't going too fast you could see the faces turning when driving past any and every car on the right lanes. It made me realise the classical, timeless beauty of this car. A timeless, beautiful woman next to me in my timeless, beautiful car. What more could I want? Ah, to visit my timeless, beautiful daughter.

"What are you smiling at?" Françoise asked.

Marie-Isobelle felt warm, even though the weather had cooled down. She was gently glowing, but wasn't yet aware of it.

Elle watched Maribelle, as she looked different, seemingly illuminated, glowing? She took her on her lap, but couldn't find anything wrong.

Joan and I watched Mai acting differently, very calm, as if she was focusing inward, and yet seemed very aware as she looked at us, while the train brought us to Amsterdam.

In Amsterdam, Eddie was waiting at Amsterdam Central station, but he wasn't with the Audi S4 I was expecting.

"It's at the workshop," he said, "an issue with the distribution chain. But they gave me this as a loan car. Not bad, eh?"

I didn't immediately recognise it.

"It's a 1984 BMW M5, freshly restored and with the latest hydrogen technology. Very amusing to drive."

"Not too amusing please, today?" I said with a smile.

I had booked a hotel close to the Dam square, centrally placed, and not too far from Françoise and Elle.

"You are glowing!" Elle said to Françoise. They both were quite surprised about it. Françoise walked to the bathroom to see for herself. It was like a gentle aura, but you could miss it if you weren't particularly looking on this bright, summery day.

"Look at yourself, and Maribelle," Françoise said, laughing.

"I think I'll ask Eddie, he knows such things," Françoise said, "but we'll meet him this evening anyhow. We'll see."

Joan and Mai looked different, radiant. I wasn't sure if anyone could see it, or if it was just me.

When we arrived at the cafe, that evening, nobody particularly watched us, so maybe indeed, not everybody could see it. Eddie was already waiting, as he had reserved a table for us, next to the window. I actually thought it was the same table as when we first had met. Not even a minute later Elle and Françoise came in, with Maribelle. I immediately noticed their appearance, gently glowing, just like I had seen with Joan and Mai. Was I the only one not glowing? In the reflection of the window though, I saw I was radiating in the same way as the others. Eddie introduced us to each other, but then again, that hardly was necessary. Everyone was so kind and considerate, it was almost scary, I thought. But soon I started to settle, calm down.

"Can I hold Mai?" Françoise asked. My heart rate jumped up again. Mai seemed completely comfortable with Françoise. With both hands she touched her face and looked her straight in the eyes. It was good, that's what it felt like. It was good.

"Are you OK?" Joan asked Françoise.

"Yes, yes, thank you," Françoise said with a lump in her throat, while she gently gave Mai back to Joan.

I dearly felt for her, and if not in this situation, I surely would have hugged her. Instead I gently squeezed her hand, while Joan approvingly nodded at me.

It took about half an hour before most of the tension had dissolved. The only one keeping a bit out of it was Elle. Not absent, but mostly observing, while holding Maribelle, who was mostly observing Mai.

There was a glow in our group, slowly pulsating, like a wave, a gentle wave, a gentle ocean.

"Shall we have a look at the observation platform, while the sun still is up?" Elle then asked.

We all looked at Elle, and we all agreed.

While most took the lift, Françoise and I took the stairs. For some reason I thought it was the right thing to do. As expected about halfway up the stairs we both took each other's hand as we moved on. In her white top and black jeans she looked absolutely stunning. I felt thrilled with emotion, I had that otherworldly feeling again. In a way naughty, in a way totally normal, and in between the stairs it almost felt like dancing. When we reached the final stair we let go, and looked around at the others. They were all looking up. Right above us a Sentinel was gently glowing, I had not seen it as low as this before. It felt as if it was connecting, with all of us. With each and every one of us. I felt connected, us, all, warm, radiant, safe, powerful, here and now, there and then, the All of it. What felt like maybe half an hour was probably just a minute in real time.

Then we went down again. This time we all took the lift. Our dinner was being served. It felt like an old family dinner.

After we all had enjoyed our deserts, we agreed to meet again tomorrow at the *Rijksmuseum*. I was so immensely relieved.

"Wanna have a ride in the M5 while it is still light?" Eddie asked me.

Joan approved.

"Have fun," she said.

While we walked along the canal to pick up his car Eddie started talking about parallel worlds, dimensional travel. We noticed the Sentinel again, hovering in the sky.

"Let's take the B-road," Eddie said, "that's easier to get some amusement out of this car. That's what makes this world so much fun, right?"

He then started accelerating, it felt like fun alright. Out of nowhere a white sports car appeared from the right. It looked exactly like my 4C. I grabbed the steering wheel to avoid a collision. Eddie seemed to have lost control of his car. From the other side a truck quickly approached us and it ran head-on into us, we were catapulted into a wall. A few minutes later I found myself being dragged out of the car. Out of the truck a man, dressed in black, climbed down.

Françoise was wearing an orange-red dress.

He slowly walked towards me. He looked at me through my eyes, I looked at him through his eyes. The headache became unbearable. The pain and blood seemed unreal and yet so real.

Then the blood was gone, no pain.

I looked up. Françoise looked more beautiful than ever.

305

Quotations.

Page 142, 260.

Johan Andreas dèr Mouw,

"Full of God and tiny pancakes. Sixteen Poems."

Page 269.

"The Emerald Tablets of Thoth." From tablet 7.